"Don't fight me, Gemma. We were lovers once...."

She could sense the contained emotion within him, even as she tried to control the mad pounding of her own heart. "Do you think I've forgotten, Thor? That I could ever forget?"

"Then don't pretend an indifference you don't feel!" he rasped. "Don't lie to me!" And his mouth encouraged her lips to part under his caress. But just as Gemma felt the world dissolving in disorder about her, he broke the embrace. "It's still there, isn't it, Gemma—the magic between us?" he asked hoarsely.

"No!" She lied, not daring to awake the fires of the past in case this time their flames consumed her entirely. "And you seem to forget I'm engaged to be married!"

"No more than you do!"

ANGELA WELLS left the bustling world of media marketing and advertising to marry and start a family in a suburb of London. Writing started out as a hobby, and she uses backgrounds she knows well from her many travels for her books. Her ambitions, she says, in addition to writing many more romances, are to visit Australia, pilot a light aircraft and own a word processing machine.

ANGELA WELLS

love's wrongs

Harlequin Books

TORONTO • NEW YORK • LONDON
AMSTERDAM • PARIS • SYDNEY • HAMBURG
STOCKHOLM • ATHENS • TOKYO • MILAN

Harlequin Presents first edition April 1989
ISBN 0-373-11164-9

Original hardcover edition published in 1988
by Mills & Boon Limited

CHAPTER ONE

IN THE act of slicing a bread stick, Gemma froze. Inside the small bar where she stood transfixed, the air was warm, unstirring. Outside the evening breeze ruffled the colourful covers of the dozen or so tables sprawled alongside the narrow, pretty inlet.

Had she been mistaken? No—she would recognise that tune anywhere. Although she hadn't heard it for five years it remained seared into her memory, filled into the dark recesses of her subconscious, no longer willingly recalled but impossible to erase.

Carefully laying down her knife, she wiped her hands methodically on some disposable tissue before making her way to the narrow doorway of the bar. It wasn't uncommon for customers to ask Leo to play their favourite songs; in fact, the skill of the young Menorcan guitarist was one of the reasons the Tramontana was so popular. Only nineteen now, he would have been a schoolboy when for three brief months the lyrical composition he was toying with had swept through the hit charts of Europe.

A stab of long-repressed pain caught at her heart, as Leo's nimble fingers caressed the strings, flirting with different keys as he became familiar with the theme, finding and settling for the melodic D flat. Every moment of every day of those particular three months would live in Gemma's memory for ever, despite the stringent efforts she'd made to eradicate the past.

Each tender moment spent in Thor's arms under the misapprehension that he loved her, that he wanted to

marry her, forced itself into her consciousness. It had
been *their* tune, echoing *their* passion, expressing
poetically what was in *their* hearts—or so she'd thought
that night when she'd given herself completely and for
the first time in absolute love to the tall, good-looking
visitor who had wooed her with such tenderness. Just
one month later her fool's paradise had been destroyed
by Thor's announcement that he had changed his mind
about marriage. He was returning to Australia by
himself.

She had learned to live with his rejection. For the most
part, she rarely thought of him nowadays. Only sometimes, when she couldn't sleep, she'd go downstairs and
sit on the terrace of the converted farmhouse she shared
with Noel, staring at the fat Spanish moon and remembering the time she'd been seventeen and innocent and
in love...

Whoever had made the request to Leo must be of that
era of her youth, with memories similar to her own—
but happier, even fulfilled. Curiosity took her through
the beaded doorway, on to the narrow frontage be-
strewn with potted plants and bay trees in pots. Her quick
gaze travelled over the remaining customers—only a few
left now as midnight approached, and by law the live
entertainment would have to stop: some German teenagers engaged in noisy conversation, a middle-aged
couple staring into space... Gemma swivelled round to
cast a practised eye in the other direction and felt a powerful surge of shock strike at her heart.

Five years later, and Thor McCabe had changed. At
twenty-five he'd been an attractive young man with his
coltish grace, tawny hair and startling light blue eyes beneath thick, straight brows. Now time had given him
maturity and a ripened masculine beauty that made
Gemma's breath catch in her throat. He sat in profile

to her, staring out across the moonlit waters, apparently deep in thought, his long, spatulate fingers tapping out the rhythm as Leo played.

She had never wanted to see him again, had thought herself secure half the globe away in this quiet corner of Menorca, and now he'd had the temerity to intrude once more on her life! Because his being there and persuading Leo to play *that* tune was certainly no coincidence! Her fingers balled into her palms, knowing she should turn away and go, but unable to tear her eyes away from the clear-cut features of the man who had shattered her teenage dreams of romance.

'Gemma!' She had left escape too late. Ignominious flight being the only alternative to cool acceptance, she forced her wooden lips into a smile of greeting. He had robbed her of so many things, but she still had her pride!

'Thor.' She jerked her dark head in a nod of acknowledgement. 'I thought I was seeing things.'

'And hearing them, too?' He was on his feet, moving towards her, as he indicated Leo with a turn of his head. 'I wondered if you'd remember our tune. Your guitarist has a good ear for music.'

How cruel could he be? She shrugged her shoulders, conscious of the way his eyes were lingering on the fine Italian cotton of her drawstring blouse. 'The melody did seem vaguely familiar,' she allowed carelessly, deliberately evading his outstretched hand. 'I must admit I didn't imagine it was your signature tune. Wouldn't "Waltzing Matilda" have been more apt?' She lifted a dark brow in amused enquiry. 'Anyway, what brings you to Europe?'

'My grandmother's funeral, for one thing...' He pulled out a chair at a nearby table. 'You can spare the time for a chat, can't you?'

'If you like. It's quiet tonight. A lot of the package tours are flying out. I expect to close down shortly after midnight.' She sat down gracefully in the proffered chair. 'I'm sorry to hear about your grandmother. It must have been quite sudden. Dad didn't mention anything about her being ill in his last letter.'

'Heart,' Thor said succinctly. 'I'm glad she didn't suffer. She was a grand old lady. My mother hates flying, and the thought of twenty-one hours in a plane was too much of an ordeal for her, so I volunteered to represent the family at the funeral. Besides,' he paused, 'I wanted to revisit Leychurch. It held a lot of happy memories...' Light eyes locked with Gemma's dark gaze, coolly enigmatic.

Stunned by the sheer callousness of his approach, she struggled for words. Five years ago this—this unfeeling *brute* had erupted into her peaceful village life, leaving his adopted land of Australia to pay a long overdue visit to his mother's mother. He had wormed his way into her father's house on the pretext of a long-distant friendship that had existed between his mother and her father before the former had married Frank McCabe and emigrated, and having been made welcome had proceeded to court, seduce and finally desert the only daughter of the house! Oh, yes, she had memories, but happy wasn't the word she would have used to describe them!

'It's a pretty enough place, I suppose.' She refused to respond to the question his eyes had asked. 'But I prefer warmer climes. My life is here on the island now.'

'Yes, your father told me about the set-up you've got. I understand you've got interests in property development and a restaurant as well as this bar?'

'Plus a few subsidiary investments in jewellery and marine engines.' She laughed naturally, glad to take the conversation away from England and the humiliation she'd suffered at Thor's hands. 'You name it, and Noel's got money in it!'

She signalled across to Leo who'd finished the song and was sitting quietly strumming the strings of his guitar. 'Bring us a bottle of champagne, please, will you?'

As the young man rose instantly to obey, Thor reached across the table to cover one of her unsuspecting hands with his own. 'Are you pleased to see me again, Gemma?' His voice was low and sweet, the lazy Australian vowels attractive to her ear. 'I wondered, perhaps...'

'If I resented the fact you found the wide open spaces more attractive than a gauche girl of seventeen?' Was it just idle curiosity that made him want to see if her wounds were still raw? Or would it give him some kind of kick to confirm how deeply the probe of his disdain had pierced? Either way, the preservation of her own pride lay in pretence.

She was pleased with the casual laugh she managed to emit. 'As a matter of fact, it was the best thing that could have happened to me. I was much too young for marriage, as you found out for yourself. Oh, at the beginning, I was serious enough, but it didn't take much time to realise after you'd left that I wasn't in love with you—simply in love with love!' She made a small moue of distaste. 'The worst thing about it was having wasted all that money on white satin for the ceremony and missing out on being the youngest bride in the village church this century!' Her acting improving by the second, she gave him a coquettish smile. 'Still, my dear Thor, I have to admit you were an admirable instructor in the art of love—but the real fun lies in practising what one's been taught, doesn't it? I'll always be grateful for your initiation, if that's what you wanted to know.'

'It wasn't!' Thor's jaw tightened ominously as the light eyes narrowed in annoyance. She felt his anger transmitted to his fingers and withdrew her hand quickly from his grasp. This was a new, more dangerous Thor, with a man's steely temper she'd never witnessed before, and it was clear he hadn't liked the flippancy of her answer; or perhaps her assertion that her love had been as fickle as his own had wounded his male conceit.

Thankfully she saw Leo approaching the table with champagne and glasses. Her emotions were see-sawing so rapidly, she didn't know what she was doing. Bitterness and hurt were mixing with the remnants of the deep love she'd once felt for this man and causing a maelstrom of feeling within her, threatening her carefully assumed composure.

When both glasses were filled, she lifted her own and clinked it against Thor's. *'Salud y pesetas,'* she intoned carelessly.

His stern mouth relaxed, *'Y el tiempo de gustarlos.'* He finished the traditional Spanish toast, and downed his glass in one long swallow, before passing thoughtful eyes over her face. 'Well, you certainly look healthy enough, blooming, in fact...' There was more than indifferent appraisal in his tone, an echo of the warmth that had once sent tingling messages of fire to every cell in her body. Gemma felt herself stiffen defensively as he continued softly, 'And I'd say you'd got plenty of time on your side to enjoy your health, but what about the *"pesetas"* part of it? It seems to me the property development side of your empire has come to a standstill. This afternoon I went up to the Cala Parangas site and found it deserted—a mere shell—with no sign of work in hand.'

'You've been trespassing!' Anger choked in her throat as Gemma rose to her feet defensively, stung by the derogatory tone she'd detected in his observation. 'What right did you have to enter private property? In any case, we do things more slowly here than in the Antipodes—after all, we've been at it much longer!'

'Sit down, Gemma, you're upsetting your customers.' The mild command halted her invective, but she remained standing, her breast heaving with the effort of controlling her temper. Her first impression that Thor had changed was being ratified by the minute. There was an added strength of purpose to his bearing, a strain of command in the deep voice she'd never noticed before.

The last five years had hardened and toughened him. Not only was that obvious in the breadth of his shoulders and the depth of his chest beneath the stretch of black cotton shirt that covered his torso, but it evidenced in the uncompromising firmness of his chin and the resolute curve of his beautiful mouth. Above his right eyebrow the long, hairline scar, the result of a power-boat accident in his native Australia when he was a child, tightened ominously as his forehead tensed. For the first time since she'd known him, Gemma felt a soupçon of fear, knowing instinctively this new Thor McCabe would be a dangerous man to cross. Beneath the cold censure of his eyes she subsided once more in her seat, aware that her heated retort had been uncalled for and furious that she hadn't been able to hide the wave of resentment his unexpected presence had conjured up in her wayward heart.

'The site was unguarded,' he commented softly, telling her what she was perfectly aware of. 'And in any case, I had a legitimate reason for looking at it.'

Conscious that the group of German teenagers were staring at her with unfeigned interest, Gemma sipped the cool, tart Spanish champagne. She was over-reacting, betraying the chaos that was churning inside her, at his sudden re-entry into her quiet, well-organized life.

'I'm sorry, Thor.' She gave him a thin smile. 'I'm not usually so aggressive. It's been a long day for me. One of the girls in the restaurant had a day off and I covered for her before coming down here. I guess I'm a little overtired.' It was as gracious an apology as she could make in the circumstances. 'What do you mean by "legitimate reason"?'

'I was considering re-financing it.' He refilled his glass before leaning back in his chair, long legs splayed out before him, to regard her dazed expression with quiet satisfaction. 'I take it that the reason work has stopped there is lack of liquidity?'

Gemma stared back into the clear blue eyes assessing her: the eyes of a man who was used to gazing across vast areas of untamed land, their vulnerability protected from the scorching rays of the Outback sun by the sweep of dark lashes which contrasted so dramatically with the sun-bleached streaks of gold in his thick, tawny hair. Now they rested on the near target of her own face, dwelling with obvious pleasure on its astonishment.

For a moment Gemma hesitated. Was he being serious? Had Thor really accumulated enough funds in the past five years to make such an offer feasible?

'You want to see my bank statement?' The light humour in his voice told her he'd read her thoughts with consummate ease. 'You can believe my interest's genuine, Gemma. I don't joke about business.'

No, only about love! She bit back her instant reaction, forcing herself to concentrate on the matter at hand. For six months Noel had been trying to raise more capital to get the project started again. Most of his money had been sunk into it, but a series of disasters had struck until the dwindling cash flow of the company had been insufficient to pay the wages. Parangas had become a frozen asset, its value decaying as time went by.

She couldn't betray Noel's confidences. She owed him far too much. If he and his sister Laura, who had been her best friend at school, hadn't welcomed her into their home and their business five years ago when she'd been near breaking point, she might never have recovered from the shock of Thor's desertion as quickly as she had. Didn't loyalty forbid her to discuss Noel's problems with the man sitting opposite her?

On the other hand, she agonised silently, the situation was patently clear to anyone with a minimal knowledge of building, and Thor had obviously done his homework! She couldn't afford to let this opportunity slip—if it was genuine. She'd have to proceed, but with caution.

'We had a bad winter, a lot of rain which held up work.' She shrugged dismissively, minimising what had been near disaster. 'Then there was a dispute on the site. The delay's only temporary, of course. Now the summer season's underway, profits from both the bar and restaurant will ease the situation, and we're waiting for settlement of a large fashion jewellery order recently sent to Paris.' Her curiosity overcame her caution. 'Why ever should *you* be interested in Parangas?'

'Expansion of existing interests.' He took a long draught of his drink. 'A great deal's happened in the last five years. When I first went back to Oz I travelled around the Outback for a while, working the wildness out of my blood by rounding up cattle. That came to a halt after I took a bit of a tumble and decided enough was enough!' His teeth flashed white against the dark tan of his smooth skin. 'I made my way to the east coast, spent a little time riding surf as a relaxation, and was fortunate enough to meet a guy who owned one of the small islands on the Reef.

'My father's eldest brother had recently died and unexpectedly left me a healthy legacy in gold-mining shares. The market was climbing, and even after duties I had enough collateral to invest in the project of turning it into a select holiday resort. Within the first year we knew we were on to a winner and we began looking for another project. It was only when my grandmother died, though, and I had to come to England that we thought of Europe.

Ed Curran, my partner, has always had a hankering for the ''Old World'', and he suggested I take the opportunity of looking round the Med. to assess possibilities.'

'And you immediately thought of Menorca?' She began to relax. It was coincidence, his being here. After all, why not? Menorca was still recognised as being fairly unspoilt. She'd been absurd to think that her presence on the island had influenced him in any way. The relief was almost tangible.

'No,' he replied calmly. 'As a matter of fact, my first thought was the Greek Isles. Then I met your father at the funeral, and he invited me back for a meal and a chat about old times...'

Oh, Dad! Gemma sighed inwardly. Robin Carson had always had a soft spot for Thor McCabe, the two men finding an instinctive affinity from their first meeting, despite the difference in their ages. At one time she'd even been arrogant enough to assume that love for *her* was the common bond they shared.

Robin Carson's affection had never been in doubt. He couldn't have loved her more if she'd been his own child, rather than the deserted waif he and his wife had adopted when she'd been abandoned by her own mother so the latter could marry a man who had no room in his life for another man's child. It had been Thor whose motives had been shallow—a summer's pleasure and then 'goodbye'.

During the nightmare days that had followed his departure, both her parents—for that was how she would regard Robin and Stella Carson, had been loving and supportive. It was better, they'd comforted her, that Thor should acknowledge his own restless nature then, rather than later, when they'd been legally tied to each other. She was young. She would forget him.

Of course, she'd never told them that she and Thor had been lovers. Even Robin's forgiving nature would have found *that* hard to come to terms with. Even now, she was uncertain why she'd spared him the knowledge of her surrender to their handsome visitor. Certainly her own pride was a tantamount reason, but there'd been something else as well... She hadn't wanted her father to suffer the same disillusionment she had undergone. He'd found pleasure in Thor's friendship. It was something she hadn't wanted to tarnish. At least her fickle lover had ensured she wouldn't become pregnant. She supposed she should be grateful for that consideration!

'Gemma?' His soft drawl penetrated her thoughts.

A dull flush coloured her cheeks. 'I'm sorry?'

'I said I was sorry to hear about your mother's death.'

'Yes.' She stared down at the table. 'She and Dad were devoted, but he took it very well. Shortly before they adopted me she was very ill, you know. She suffered what's known as an ectopic pregnancy. At one time she nearly died. Even afterwards Dad said he counted every day they spent together as a bonus.' She paused, conscious of Thor's quiet sympathy. 'I went back for the funeral, of course. In fact, I was all set to stay in England, but Dad wouldn't hear of it. You see, Laura had recently married a Spanish boy and gone back to Barcelona with him, and Noel and I were on our own, with business really taking off. Dad was most insistent I came back to Menorca.'

She spoke the truth, but still a feeling of guilt nagged at her. Her adoptive father had showered so much love on her, fought so many battles on her behalf as she grew up, as if he'd always been trying to compensate for her first traumatic rejection by her natural mother, that she still wondered if she should have overridden his instructions to return to Menorca and stayed by his side. On the other hand, he'd always been the physically stronger of her parents, taking full responsibility for the household management...

'A wise decision.' Thor's approval seemed genuine. 'He was certainly in the best of spirits when I saw him. When I told him what I was considering, he told me of the partnership you have with Noel and the plans you both have for Parangas and asked me why I didn't consider Menorca instead of Greece. The more I thought about it, the better the idea seemed. East or West Mediterranean—it made no difference to me, but to have a site already selected and plans drawn up...well...' he paused meaningfully. '...it would mean a much earlier completion and commencement of returns. Besides...' this time the pause was longer, as Gemma found herself unable to meet his gaze '...I thought it would be an opportunity to renew an old friendship.'

With hands that shook, Gemma eased her chair away from the table. How dared he use that bait on her after what he'd done to her? If he'd turned her down for another woman she might have understood better, but to be deserted for a load of cattle was degrading! And the cruel way in which he'd broken the news of his decision to her gave him no right to speak of friendship!

Almost certainly he was married by now, with a brood of children running wild on his paradise island. He'd wanted to see her, had he? Well, *he* was the last person *she'd* ever wished to set eyes on again! For all *she* cared he could go back Down Under tomorrow and leave her in her own paradise without his serpentine presence to distract her!

On the point of putting her thoughts pithily into words, she hesitated. In the first place, for the sake of her own self-esteem, she'd just denied any feelings of antipathy towards him, hadn't she? And in the second, despite his efforts to hide it from her, Noel was a worried man. Only by clever juggling of his resources had he managed to keep Tramontana and the restaurant, La

Langousta, in the black. Any day now that situation could alter, with drastic effect on the small staff employed.

In the past, Noel's Spanish business partner—a legal necessity for a non-Spanish national—had bailed him out. Recently, help from Madrid had not been so easily forthcoming. Ramón Casados had begun to hoard his *pesetas* for a rainy day, and it was no secret he regarded the Parangas Development with less than optimism.

Biting her lower lip, Gemma rose to her feet. If Thor genuinely intended to put money into the project, surely it was her duty to encourage him to do so? The very least she could do would be to arrange a meeting between him and Noel. What was there to lose?

'Where are you going?' In an instant Thor was with her as she turned from the table.

'To fetch a pencil and paper and draw you a map of where you can find Noel,' she told him calmly. 'Whatever you have in mind, you'll have to discuss it with him personally. He might be prepared to give you a bite of the apple, but it will be *his* decision—not mine.'

Conscious of his close presence, she gained the inside of the bar, insinuating herself behind the narrow counter and reaching for a pencil and order pad. 'Noel owns a converted farmhouse on the outskirts of San Luis.' She glanced up as she felt his blue gimlet gaze boring into her. 'Where are you staying on the island?'

'I've rented a villa in El Dorado—the Villa Sabina—overlooking the golf course.' He named one of the island's most exclusive resort settlements. 'I daresay you know of it. It's a few miles outside Mahón.'

'I've heard of it,' Gemma countered drily. 'I understand it's slightly more ambitious than Parangas. Your best route is to go through Mahón and follow the signposts to San Luis. This is your route from the crossroads.' She tore the sheet from the order pad and presented it to him. 'He's there most mornings. After ten is best.'

'Tomorrow, then.' He took the slip of paper from her. There were no rings on his hands, she noted, but then that proved nothing. Few of the male sex advertised their responsibilities, especially when they looked like Thor McCabe. Idly she wondered how many women had known him as intimately as she had. The self-inflicted pain of the supposition was more severe than she'd expected. She felt herself flinch.

'Gemma...'

She'd been so immersed in her own thoughts that she was unprepared for the sudden movement he made. Unexpectedly she found her shoulders grasped as Thor reached across the narrow bar.

'You've changed, Gemma...' In the dim light of the interior his light eyes were still a force to be reckoned with, as they swept over her face. 'Your hair used to be long, shoulder-length...' He touched the soft feather cut of nut-brown silk that clung to her shapely head, fringed on her forehead and curled seductively in the nape of her neck.

'It's cooler this way.' Her voice was husky, the rapid pulse-beat in her throat betraying her agitation. Where was Leo? All the customers had gone and, from the neatness all around her, the young Menorcan had already cleared up ready for the morning. But he'd never go without telling her...

'It's beautiful.' Lean, strong fingers touched the softly flicked curls. 'It makes your eyes look even larger—soft and luminous—like a doe's.' Gemma drew in a breath, unable to speak as he traced the line of her cheek. 'You're slimmer, too. All these years I've remembered you as enchantingly pretty, but now, *now*, Gemma—you're beautiful.' The tracing finger wandered to her mouth and began to follow the outline of her lips.

'No, Thor!' She tried to pull away but was swamped by his strength, finding herself held rigid against the bar as he leaned towards her. 'Please, Thor...' Her throat was abnormally dry, the words little more than a croak. Five years ago, with her adolescent plumpness and naïveté, she'd been beddable rather than marriageable, but if he thought they could start where they'd left off, if he fancied another brief summer affair, he would have to think again!

'Is it really five years, Gemma?' His voice was husky with suppressed emotion. 'It seems like only yesterday...' Effortlessly he pulled her to him, branding her with the hot passion of his kiss, and time telescoped. Gemma was seventeen once more, desperately in love, full of trust and adoration for the handsome Australian who had entered her small world and filled it with his exuberance and desire. Lost in her memories, she let her mouth flower beneath his caress, accepting it without restraint as her hands reached to his shoulders. She was oblivious of the hard rim of the bar pressing into her ribs, and all her sensations in that instant were centred round Thor—the scent and taste of him, the pressure of his lips devouring her, the warm, muscular presence of his flesh beneath her fingers.

The bead curtain parted with a soft jangle. 'If you have no further need of me I'll be going...' Leo stopped uncomfortably on the threshold.

Instantly Gemma tensed, a flush of shame staining her cheeks as Thor reluctantly released her.

'Thank you, Leo.' It was little more than a whisper as she fought to conquer the flood of weakness which threatened to floor her. Dear heavens, what had she allowed to happen? Her only consolation was that the barrier of the bar had prevented Thor's body from seeking as intimate a knowledge of her as his marauding mouth.

'Can I drive you home, Gemma? Where do you live?' Thor waited until Leo had left before asking the question. 'My car's parked at the top of the cliff road.'

'Thank you, no.' She was proud of her cool reply. 'I have a motor scooter parked at the back. It's ideal for these roads.' She made to walk briskly past him, but was forestalled by his arm on her shoulder.

'Don't touch me!' She fired at him with a cold fury, her heart-shaped face tight with displeasure.

'I'm sorry...' The offending hand was removed, as his voice became coolly formal. 'Please forgive me, Gemma. I had no right to jump on you like that.' Her mouth warm from his kiss, the blood throbbing in her veins, Gemma knew she was facing a fight for survival against the powerful presence of a man who would always be able to bend her to his will unless she used every atom of mental and physical reserve she had. Not again, oh, not again, dear lord, would she suffer willingly at his faithless hands! What could her father have been thinking about to betray her present whereabouts to this knave of hearts?

'No, you didn't, Thor.' Gemma took a step away from him, watching with cool disdain the frown that marred the smooth expanse of his broad forehead. 'What happened five years ago is water under the bridge.' She shrugged. 'A passing interlude put down to experience and forgotten. Besides, as I've already explained, I think my father must have given you the wrong impression of my relationship with Noel. Although I work for him, we're not business partners. The kind of partnership we share is more intimate.' Her voice shook slightly. 'Ever since his sister married and went to the mainland, Noel and I have been living together at the farmhouse.' She saw with painful satisfaction the shock register on Thor's face, almost as if she had reached out and slapped its taut outline, but he hadn't heard everything she meant to impart.

With casual nonchalance, she took down the heavy key to the front door from its hook and motioned Thor to leave the building before her. Once outside, she turned it in the lock with meticulous attention, testing the door before pocketing the key in the hip pocket of her jeans. Only then did she turn to face him.

In the moonlight the blond streaks in his hair gleamed silver, the strong bones of his face were highlighted, the tense lines of his athletic body poised for action. A shiver trembled through her. The old magic was still there, intensified even, but this time she wouldn't fall for it. Never again would she endanger her heart, her soul and her body to his meretricious charm. This time she would use every protection she had at hand.

'Come October,' she told him coolly, 'when the season's over, Noel and I are going back to England to be married in the village church at Leychurch.'

He was still standing there, motionless, as she collected her motor scooter and stabbed it into vibrating life. Reaching the top of the narrow path that led from the inlet to the larger track at the top of the cliff, she headed toward the main road without looking back once.

CHAPTER TWO

'MARRIED!' Noel Shelton regarded Gemma with blank astonishment, as his hand reached out toward the percolator. 'Good God, Gem, I'm flattered, of course, but it seems a bit drastic!' Casually dressed and unshaven, he peered at her across the breakfast table set on the shaded terrace. 'I can't pretend that any offer of investment isn't welcome, but not at the cost of your peace of mind. If this Aussie guy poses any kind of threat to you, then...'

'It's not quite like that, Noel.' Gemma searched his pleasant face for signs of annoyance and discovered only surprise. She uttered a small sigh of relief. For the past five years Noel had been like a brother to her. Four years her senior, charming, unassuming and incredibly untidy, he was her best friend now Laura had left. The arrangement of sharing the house worked extremely well, with Gemma acting as housekeeper and Noel footing the expenses. She would have hated to have offended him.

'I've told you I knew him in England—the fact is, Thor McCabe was the man who asked me to marry him and then jilted me.' Even now, saying the words reawakened the hurt. Both Laura and Noel had known what had happened, but she'd never gone into details and they'd never pried. Now she owed it to Noel to be frank.

'*That* bastard!' He glowered at her, a lock of dark hair falling boyishly across his forehead. 'Hell, Gem, I don't want anything to do with a guy like that.'

24

Touched by his concern, she smiled. 'Be realistic, Noel. Thor's money's as good as anyone else's—probably better, because he's had experience in this kind of thing. And what happened between us was a long time ago, and probably for the best. After all, I was only an impressionable teenager, and Thor was eight years older. At that time in my life it was an enormous age gap— the distance between a child and an adult. If we had got married it would never have lasted, and divorce would have been messy and protracted, whereas Thor's sudden decision had the cleanness and efficiency of a surgeon's knife.' And the pain of the latter used without an-aesthetic, she acknowledged in silent agony. But she knew the arguments off by heart, had recited them enough times in the lonely darkness of her bed in the early days, and still she wasn't entirely persuaded by them. She'd been young, but she hadn't been stupid. She'd been in-experienced, but not ignorant. With the total com-mitment she'd been prepared to give, she might have made it work!

'If you're so happy about the situation, why tell him you and I were going to get married?' Noel's dark gaze challenged her. 'You must have felt you needed more than the protection of a friend?'

'I...' She stared down at her slim ringless fingers. 'It was just a feeling I got.' She raised her troubled eyes to Noel's brooding gaze. 'Thor McCabe's a born winner. The kind of man who goes looking for challenges. I swear he would never have considered Menorca if Dad hadn't told him something about Parangas. He was probably a little indiscreet, and Thor knew before he came here that we were in trouble, and saw the ideal opportunity of getting in on the ground floor for maximum profit-ability. The thing is—*I* don't want to become another challenge to him, and it's just possible that if I was free he might try and resurrect the past on a temporary basis just to prove I'm not immune to his special brand of allure.'

'You're still in love with him?' The gentle question was typical of Noel's insight. 'Is that why you've never formed another relationship—God knows, you've had enough opportunities here during the summer!'

'You seem to forget I don't have much time to myself during the summer!' she remonstrated with a quick lift of her head. 'No, I'm not still in love with Thor McCabe. How could I be after the way he walked out? It wasn't as if I ever pressurised him into getting married. It was his idea from the start!' She blinked away unexpected tears of chagrin.

It was nearly true. She didn't love Thor. How could she, after the way he'd treated her? But he'd been her first, her only lover, and that was something she could never forget.

'Yet you'd be quite happy for him to invest in Parangas?'

'Why not?' Gemma lifted a slim shoulder. 'It's under-capitalised at the moment, but it's sound enough. Why shouldn't you benefit from his largesse? Knowing Thor, you won't see a *peseta* until he's satisfied he'll get a return for his money. And I don't anticipate he'll hang around here for long. He's like a swallow—a temporary summer visitor!' She was ashamed of the bitterness in her voice. The last comment had been meant to sound amusing. From the pity on Noel's face, she knew her intention had failed.

'OK, if that's what you want, Gem, I'll certainly talk to him.' He shot her a mischievous look. 'And I guess I'd better get used to calling you "sweetheart".'

'You honestly don't mind pretending we're engaged?' Gemma's conscience stirred uneasily. 'It was a dreadful liberty to take, I know, but since there's no one special in your life at the moment...' She stopped in response to Noel's lifted eyebrows.

'I didn't realise you followed my personal life so vividly.' The slight edge in the comment appalled her as she felt the warm blood rise to her cheeks.

'Well, I don't,' she hastened to assure him. 'Only, after Inga went back to Sweden last year you haven't been...' She stopped in confusion, relieved when he grinned at her.

'It's all right. I'll make sure no jealous girlfriend will cut your throat in the dark. Oh, lord...' His face grimaced as the ring of the phone pierced the still morning air. 'Who can that be so early?'

He rose lazily from the table, an intensely likeable young man, a bit of a drifter who hadn't perhaps used his family inheritance to the best advantage, but an honest man and a loyal friend. Why on earth hadn't she given her heart to someone like Noel?

A few minutes later he was back, helping himself to one of the delicious sweetbread buns from the basket on the table.

'There's been a slight change of plan,' he told Gemma laconically. 'Instead of McCabe coming here this morning, we're invited to lunch at the Villa Sabina.'

'*We?*' she echoed in dismay. 'But I'd no intention of being here when he called. I was going to the market in Mahón!'

'Can't it wait?' Noel fingered the stubble on his chin with long, sensitive fingers. 'He was most adamant—"you and your lovely fiancée" was what he said!'

Damn the man! He must have known she would try to avoid him after last night. Gemma could have wept with frustration.

'I can call the whole thing off if you prefer it.' Noel's generous offer boosted her determination. Good grief! She was no longer a trusting seventeen-year-old with egg

on her face and her head in the clouds. She was twenty-
two years old, supervising two popular establishments
on one of the most sought after holiday resorts in the
world. She was the mistress of her own destiny, wasn't
she, quite capable of meeting Thor McCabe as a business
acquaintance without succumbing to his practised wiles?
To back out now would be to admit to a vulnerability
she no longer possessed!

She shrugged her slender shoulders. 'No, it's just
mildly inconvenient. What time are we expected?'

'Around midday for pre-lunch drinks.' His eyes were
bright with sudden devilment. 'Wear something pretty—
and don't be late, darling!' He ladled honey over the
endearment and went out of the room, an amused grin
on his boyish face.

El Dorado was a jewel. Set in wooded countryside about
two miles inland from a wide sweep of beach, the development consisted of elegant, expensive villas dotted
around seemingly haphazardly, many of which overlooked a large inland lake which was also a bird sanctuary. Known locally as a millionaire's hideaway with
its tennis courts and nine-hole golf course, rented
property didn't come cheap.

The whole ambience reinforced Gemma's first opinion
that Thor McCabe had money to spend. Six years ago
all he'd had was ambition. She wondered idly if he would
have flourished so much if he'd stood by his offer of
marriage to her, and had to admit that it was unlikely.

'Here we are.' Noel halted their small car suddenly as
they turned sharply in the narrow, winding road to enter
a concealed driveway.

The Villa Sabina was beautiful. A long, arched
veranda surmounted by a tiled roof ran the length of
the front of the building. From the centre of this, but
confined to the centre third of the structure, was a second

storey. As she alighted from the car, Gemma's eyes swept
with appreciation over the elegant lines of the villa with
its traditionally white-painted walls and its flight of stone
steps to one side, presumably leading to a flat roof at
the rear of the house.

While Noel gathered together the portfolio he'd
brought along for the purpose of discussion, Gemma
gazed around the surrounding garden. Oleanders and
hibiscus were planted in groups, together with tall yucca
trees, making pools of cool shade on well-tended grass.
Beyond this she could see a kidney-shaped swimming
pool set in a paved area to one side of a low flight of
stairs leading to the veranda, around the pillars of which
climbing roses entwined with dark blue ipomoea.

The fine mist of a large garden spray playing lazily
on the grass caused rainbow patterns to reflect from the
white walls, momentarily distracting her attention as she
followed Noel towards the entrance.

It wasn't until they were halfway towards the house
that she saw the luxury sun-bed beside the pool and re-
alized their host was already outside to greet them.

Her breath caught in her throat as Thor McCabe
slowly unwound his magnificent body and walked lazily
towards them. Thankful that she was wearing dark sunglasses, Gemma allowed herself the painful pleasure of
looking at him as he moved with the easy grace of an
athlete, poised and graceful. He was wearing plain, dark
bathing shorts, the ratio of leg length to body height still
lending him the coltish appearance she remembered so
well. But there was nothing else of the adolescent about
Thor. His was a man's body, its smooth, muscular development suggesting he was as well tuned to action as
the hunters who had been his biological predecessors.

Stop it! she warned herself. To think like this was
dangerous. The days when she'd lain in Thor's arms and

been pleasured by his body were in the past. They must never be resurrected!

'Thor McCabe.' He'd come within greeting distance, announcing his name and extending a firm hand towards her companion.

'Noel Shelton.' Noel clasped the outstretched hand as he introduced himself.

'And Gemma, of course.' Thor turned his gaze towards her, magnetic blue eyes, their impact only slightly muted by the softness of the surrounding curl of dark lashes, taking in her appearance from head to foot. She'd dressed simply, a plain white cotton sleeveless sweater dress, loosely tie-belted, setting off her pale golden tan. Only when Thor's presumptuous appraisal travelled admiringly over her did she consider she might have been better advised to wear something which didn't follow the shapely curves of her slender body so faithfully!

She'd forgotten how his lingering gaze used to set fire to her blood, was furious to find that some inner remnant of her dead emotions could still stir beneath its passage. When he placed his arm round her shoulders, she felt her whole body grow tense.

'Hello again, Thor,' she said quietly, her stiff lips trying to form a polite smile for the sake of convention. It had been no more than a friendly caress, perfectly proper in front of the man he supposed to be her fiancé, but the touch of his palm on her shoulder, the sight of his barely covered body, the expression on his attractive face—half friendly, half mocking—had been enough to arouse further the memories she *had* to forget.

Instantly she became defensive, slipping away from his touch. 'I hadn't realised it was to be an informal lunch. I would have brought my bikini.'

'I'm sorry.' He was instantly apologetic. 'I should have mentioned the villa has a pool. I'd have been delighted for both of you to enjoy it.' His glance included Noel in the invitation. 'As it is, I won't make you envious by sitting around like this.' His amused glance flicked back to Gemma. 'Come up to the villa and have a drink.'

He led them towards the veranda, comfortably furnished with upholstered patio furniture, a long, low table and reclining chairs. Indicating that they seat themselves, he continued towards the interior glass doors, opened to reveal another room which obviously contained a bar.

'Still drinking Cinzano and soda, Gemma?' he called back over his shoulder. A little shiver trembled down her bare arms. Dear God—he still remembered what had once been her favourite drink!

'Did I ever?' She forced a false note of enquiry into her reply, refusing to acknowledge the efficiency of his memory. 'These days I drink gin and tonic—if you have it.'

'Of course. How about you, Noel?' Thor's narrowed gaze rested speculatively on the younger man.

'Gin suits me fine.' Noel was already taking the portfolio and brochures from his briefcase and laying them on the table as Thor returned with a tumbler in each hand. Approvingly Gemma noted that he followed the continental custom of turning the drink into a long, refreshing glassful, liberally supplied with chunks of ice and slices of lemon.

'And now, if you'll excuse me, I'll go and change.' He disappeared from the room.

'Well, that wasn't too bad for starters, was it, Gemma? He seems quite a decent guy.' Noel relaxed in the comfortable chair, his face alight with expectation.

'He's what's known as a man's man, I believe.' She took a long, cold sip from her glass. So far Thor had shown only the carefree charm that reflected one side of his character. Noel could still be in for a rougher ride than he anticipated!

Within a few minutes he rejoined them, having changed into marginally more respectable dark blue shorts and a pale blue sports shirt of a cotton so fine it was almost transparent. Gemma's eyes, relieved of sunglasses in the comparative coolness of the veranda, were drawn inexorably to the muscled stretch of bronzed thigh, with its soft dusting of golden hair, as he sank down in a chair at her side.

'It's called a "Queensland tan",' he drawled, much to her mortification, as he followed the path of her eyes. His soft laugh only adding to her discomfort as she felt her face colour with embarrassment, she deliberately evaded his scrutiny. 'Now then, Noel, let's see what you have to offer. The sooner we get started, the sooner we can have lunch, up on the roof.'

'We're actually going to eat here?' Gemma was glad to change the subject. Somehow she hadn't seen Thor going in for self-catering.

He read her dubiety and laughed. 'I'm quite capable of looking after myself and providing an edible meal for guests, but I'll forgive you for doubting it because it so happens one of the girls from the village has come in today to organise it for me. I think you may know her. Her brother's the guitarist at Tramontana.'

'Josephina? Yes, of course I know her.' She smiled in genuine pleasure. 'She's helped out at La Langousta before now. She's an excellent cook!'

'Then the sooner we get through this, the better!' He leant forward and helped himself to the bound portfolio on the table. 'Where do we start?'

For the next couple of hours Gemma sat silently, watching the two men discuss the urbanisation project so close to Noel's heart. There was no doubt about Thor's shrewdness as he asked all the right questions, and some of the wrong ones, too, judging from Noel's growing nervousness.

Watching them, it was impossible not to compare their approach. Noel was enthusiastic, if a little too optimistic about some of his conjectures. It was clear he enjoyed what he was doing and he put the advantages over well. Thor was calmer, more controlled and judgemental in his appraisal. He wasn't going to be an easy man to convince. A pang of sympathy wrung her heart. Talk of the lamb sitting down to lunch with the lion!

'I'm afraid this must be boring for you.' Thor, replenishing her glass for the second time, raised the dark bar of his eyebrows, demanding a response.

'On the contrary, I don't find Noel's business in the least bit boring!' she informed him tartly.

'Forgive me, Gemma...' But he didn't sound in the least repentant. 'I didn't mean to imply a lack of interest on your part. I meant you must be bored by the repetition of facts with which you must be well acquainted.' The words were gentle enough, but the sardonic look accompanying them left her in no doubt as to his opinion of her grasp of the intricacies under discussion. An opinion which was well deserved, if she were honest.

'I was going to suggest,' he continued smoothly, denying her the opportunity of retort, 'that if you'd like to look over the villa, please feel free to do so.'

It wasn't such a bad idea at that, she supposed, looking at the papers strewn out on the table. 'Well,' she said slowly, 'I wouldn't mind having a word with Josephina, if you've no objections.'

'Of course not. The kitchen's the second door on the left.' He indicated its location. 'Ask her to show you around.'

Nodding her thanks, Gemma followed his directions.

'Hi—need any help?' She poked her dark head round the door.

'Hello, Gemma.' The Spanish girl returned her smile. An excellent cook, she often provided and served food to the owners of the growing colony of luxury villas when they felt too lazy to look after themselves or go out for a meal. Trust Thor McCabe to get his creature comforts organised so promptly! she opined silently. It was clear to her now that Thor had been on the island for a longer time than she'd at first supposed, delaying his approach until he was satisfied Noel had something positive to offer.

'No, thanks, everything's ready.' Brightly, Josephina declined her offer. 'I'm just waiting for Señor McCabe to ask me to serve.'

'Oh, well, he suggested you might like to give me a tour of the place, then.'

'Oh, Gemma, I don't know.' Josephina looked confused. 'I'd rather be here in case he wants me, but...' She brightened. 'I'll show you where you're going to eat. Follow me.'

Gemma followed, finding herself climbing the stone steps which led, as she'd previously guessed, to a flat roof, covering the lower storey of the house, also accessed, she noted, by shuttered glass doors leading directly into what must be an upstairs bedroom.

A large awning stretched out from the house, casting a band of deep, cool shade, beneath which a long, glass-topped table was already prepared with cutlery, table mats, napkins and glasses, two white china bowls of roses lending added colour.

Potted plants and shrubs abounded, giving beauty and perfume to the whole area, but it was the view that captured Gemma's attention. From this angle the Villa Sabina overlooked the peaceful lake, set like a sapphire, reflecting the colour of the sky, its outline indeterminable, masked as it was by the bordering trees. Here there were no roads. Just the bird sanctuary and utter peace.

For several minutes the two girls indulged in desultory conversation. Then Gemma shook her head wonderingly. 'I can understand what pleasure Thor must get from this . . .' The words were little more than a whisper.

'Can you? Good.' The unexpected sound of his voice directly behind her made her jump. 'I think we can begin, when you're ready.' He tossed the direction to Josephina, who scurried away, instantly obedient.

'Cold?' Thor had seen the shudder of shock she'd tried to suppress at his sudden appearance. He knew perfectly well she wasn't cold in a temperature of eighty degrees plus, but his voice was solicitous as he took advantage of the question to put his hand on her bare shoulder.

There was nothing improper about it, but she felt as if he'd branded her. Perhaps his touch only appeared more intimate because Noel wasn't there to see it, or perhaps a woman always responded to the man who'd first awakened her self-knowledge. If so, and if she was to see more of Thor, she would have to learn to control the reaction of her body to his proximity. She must teach it to act in accordance with her mind and emotions!

Again she shivered, throwing off his embrace.

'Noel's a jealous lover, then, is he?' he drawled infuriatingly.

'I don't like being touched!' Her voice was harsh with reproach.

'No?' His tone was politely disbelieving, and she could have kicked herself for saying something so trite.

'What I mean is . . .' She started to hunt for an explanation.

'What you mean is you don't like being touched by me . . .' Thor hesitated just long enough before adding '. . . now.'

'If you like.' She was too agitated to formulate a denial. 'I really don't want to discuss the matter.'

'But I do, Gemma. In fact, there are a lot of matters I want to discuss with you...' He moved purposefully towards her, his jaw set stubbornly.

What might have happened next she could only surmise, as the sound of Noel's tread on the steps mingled with Josephina's soft voice and with a murmur of annoyance Thor turned away from her.

Vastly relieved, Gemma took her seat at the table, more thankful than ever that she'd managed to persuade Noel to play the part of her fiancé. She'd been badly hurt in the past, and she was willing to take part of the blame for what she'd suffered. History was full of men who'd persuaded women to share their beds under the promise of marriage, and she'd gone to Thor willingly— perhaps too willingly, she admitted to herself as Josephina served the first course of pâté with garlic bread. Dear heavens, but she'd been an easy conquest! Little wonder his victory had palled so soon.

She took a sip of the light, dry, white Spanish wine with which she'd been served, aware that her two male companions were talking amicably to each other. In retrospect she could forgive Thor McCabe for breaking her heart, for abandoning her with a drawer in her bedroom containing twenty yards of white satin as a constant reminder of what he had promised. She'd been young and naïve, no match for the golden-limbed man whose life she'd shared for such a brief period.

He'd taught her a painful lesson and she'd learned it well. No man had ever been allowed to approach her so closely since, either physically or emotionally. No man ever would. Certainly not the lazy-voiced Australian whose presence was already disturbing her hard-won equilibrium.

Fried chicken followed, served with a delicious salad, including grapes and orange segments with the island's famous *salsa mahonesa* freshly prepared and presented in a silver bowl. It was only after the meal had been completed with locally made ice-cream and portions of the flat, dry, Menorcan cheese, presented traditionally on a plate by itself without bread or biscuits, that Thor produced a bottle of Carlos Primero cognac.

Noel accepted the brandy, savouring the exquisite and expensive Spanish cognac with a connoisseur's appreciation. Gemma declined the offer gracefully. What with the pre-lunch drinks and the wine she felt pleasantly relaxed and drowsy, glad to be in the shade as the heat of the day burned down on to the outside world.

'Well, now. To business.' Thor pushed his chair back from the table, stretching his long legs lethargically and holding his glass up to the light.

Beside her, Gemma felt Noel stiffen. Suddenly she realised just how much Noel wanted—no, *needed*, the other man's involvement. At times, Noel's air of complacency could be misleading, as he tended to keep his worries to himself. She suspected, with a twinge of conscience, she'd been too busy lately to see just how concerned he was about the future.

'I'll be honest with you.' The uncompromising words offered little hope, as Thor met Noel's eyes squarely. 'You haven't tried to disguise your present difficulties from me and I accept that they're short-term—however, it does mean that your present need is urgent, not to say, desperate.'

Desperate? Gemma stole a look at Noel's face. Would he deny the use of such an emotive word? His face paled, but he sat there quite still, saying nothing.

'The site's ideal. I find the layout, with a few minor reservations, well-planned and attractive. However...' he paused to sip his brandy reflectively. 'Every day costs are escalating, and I'm not convinced that what you're offering is different enough or exciting enough to make it a worthwhile proposition in the long term.'

A thread of anger tightened deep inside Gemma. Wasn't it enough he'd once humiliated her? Was it Thor's plan to do the same thing to Noel? To play a cat and mouse game with him, chasing him into corners before walking disdainfully away? It was too great a price to pay—even for such a splendid meal!

It was that word 'desperate' that had reduced the situation from one of commercial bargaining to one of begging. She hadn't meant to interfere, but how could she sit here feeling the burden of Noel's despair while Thor, glorying in his ostentatious wealth, belittled him?

'Well, do you want to invest or not?' Abruptly she pushed her chair away from the table, rising to her feet, her voice brittle. 'Our situation might seem desperate to you, but Noel's lived in and around these islands for the greater part of his life. He has many friends here and on the mainland who would be only too willing to invest if we gave them the opportunity.'

She drew in a deep breath, her dark eyes flaming fury at the lounging figure of their tormentor. 'We didn't approach *you*! You came to us. Yes, we're in business and capital investment is always welcome, but we haven't come here caps in hand!' Nobly she nailed her colours to Noel's mast. 'We've shown you our project...' Her arms swept open, palms raised. 'OK—either you like it or you don't...'

'Gemma...' Noel's arm came round her shaking shoulders as he rose to calm her. 'Darling, it's all right. Don't you think you're over-reacting a little?'

She refused to answer as angry tears threatened to fall, but she allowed Noel to guide her back into her chair.

'I'm sorry.' With a feeling of utter chagrin, Gemma heard Noel's apology on her behalf. 'It's just that Gem's

more worried about my financial security than she need
be.'

'That's quite understandable—after all, you are going
to become husband and wife.' Bland and self-controlled,
his voice totally devoid of the rage she'd hoped to invoke,
Thor smiled at Gemma indulgently. 'However, your
fiancée did rather jump to conclusions. If she'd let me
finish what I was saying, she might not have reacted so
strongly.'

Beneath the gleaming white smile turned on her,
Gemma felt her skin crawl. She made an airy gesture
with one slim hand. 'Please do continue.'

'Right.' Thor's voice resumed its earlier briskness.
'What I was going to say was that, while I like your
projects, they're not unique. Similar developments are
taking place right through the Med. What I need to be
convinced about is why I should invest money here, in
this place, on this island. What are its special attrac-
tions—what magic does it have—why will the tourists
continue to come?'

Noel frowned. 'You mean you want more time to get
to know the island?'

'Yes, you could say that.' Thor topped up Noel's glass.
'What I had in mind was a guided tour by someone who
knows it really well. Someone prepared to show me its
heart as well as its history.'

Noel's face brightened. 'I'd willingly do that!'

'Ah...' Thor regarded him solemnly. 'But research
tells us that it is the woman who chooses the holiday
destination in most cases. I need to know why a woman
would want to bring her family here—the female angle.'
He paused, then added brightly, 'I thought perhaps
Gemma?'

'No!' She swallowed her dismay. No way was she
willingly going to seek this man's company. On the other
hand, she couldn't prejudice Noel's chances. 'I mean,

I'm not an experienced guide,' she qualified her bleak refusal. 'You can go on excellent tours arranged by the local tourist agency. Or you can simply buy a good tourist book and set out by yourself. It's a very small island. Within a week you could know it intimately.'

Why not? her heart screamed silently as she watched his reaction. After all, it had taken only eight weeks for him to know *her* intimately. If he could overcome a woman's scruples in so short a period, a small island should be a walkover!

'I don't like official tours—I like to get off the beaten track. And it's not much fun going out by oneself with just a map for company.' Thor waited expectantly.

Beside her, Gemma could feel Noel's growing embarrassment at her silence. What was she so scared about? Thor McCabe wasn't going to take her to some lonely cove and rape her! This was just a game to him, an amusing *divertissement* at the most. She would be her own worst enemy if she let him suspect how ambivalent her feelings were towards him.

Forcing her pretty mouth into a winning smile, she turned to the man at her side. 'Do you want me to do it, darling?' she enquired sweetly of Noel.

He took his cue perfectly. 'It's OK with me, sweetheart—if you can find the time.' His arm moved possessively round her shoulders as, impulsively, she lifted her face towards him. When, to her surprise, he dropped an affectionate kiss on her mouth, she felt a warm wave of gratitude towards him.

With Noel's arm still clasping her shoulders, the imprint of his lips still warm on her own, she looked across the table into Thor's coolly appraising gaze.

'Is tomorrow morning too early to make a start?'

CHAPTER THREE

'HAVE I kept you waiting?'

Gemma had dressed in jeans and a scarlet and white striped T-shirt, her feet comfortable in rope-soled flatties. Her aim had been to look neat and efficient, since that was the attitude she intended to take with her unwanted protégé. She'd arranged to meet Thor on Mahón's harbour front, and now here he was ahead of her at the rendezvous, rising lazily from the bollard on which he'd been perched, his charming smile well in evidence.

Dressed casually in jeans and a plain blue T-shirt, his neat waistband girded by a slim, embossed leather belt, he came towards her, the smooth-fitting jeans emphasising the muscular length of his legs.

'Not at all.' He answered her question amicably. 'We're both early. I've been watching that large steamer dock.'

Gemma's quick glance encompassed the inner island packet boat. 'The *Ciudad de Ibiza*...' she nodded. 'Beautiful, isn't she? She's one of the ferries going between the islands and Barcelona. It's quite a sight when one leaves the harbour at night, especially if you're sitting on the terrace of one of the waterside hotels in Villa Carlos. The ship comes out lit up like Regent Street at Christmas, and you feel you can put out a hand and stroke her as she passes.' She made no attempt to hide the affection she felt for the graceful, white-painted ships and their moorage.

'You love this place, don't you?' Thor had seen the sparkle of her eyes. 'Will you and Noel return here after the wedding?'

'Yes, I do love it, and I hope you'll come to feel the same way.' Studiously she refrained from answering the second part of the question, relieved when he didn't press it.

'So that I agree to invest in Parangas?'

'So you realise what it can offer—yes. Isn't that what this tour's all about?'

'One of the reasons—but there are others.'

'Well, let's hope I prove as good a guide as you anticipate.' She refused to rise to his bait, turning briskly away, indicating that he accompany her. 'The port's as good a place as any to begin. I thought we'd walk along the waterfront and climb up the steps from the harbour to the town itself.'

Thor bowed to her in mock deference. 'You're the expert, Gemma.'

She'd planned a careful itinerary, including the Archaeological and Fine Arts Museum—where Thor displayed an unexpected knowledge of Menorca's ancient conquerors, causing her to doubt gravely his assumed ignorance of the island—the Church of Santa Maria with its magnificent Austrian organ, and the ancient gateway of San Roque in the medieval remains of the old walls of the city. She took him through the narrow side streets, built to protect the inhabitants from the cold winds that could flay the capital in winter, showing him hidden corners ablaze with flowers and breathtaking views of the harbour below.

It was midday by the time they were making their way through the main shopping centre with its high-fashion shops and tourist stores, its exotic florists and attractive *patisseries* towards a fountain-dominated square, where Gemma suggested they stopped for a coffee.

'Well?' she asked brightly after he'd agreed to her suggestion and they were seated beneath a scarlet sun umbrella. 'What do you think so far?'

'That you've changed since the last time I saw you. You're more in command of your own life, less overtly sensitive to life's slings and arrows, but still more than capable of stealing a man's heart, whether he wants to lose it or not!' came the prompt reply.

It wasn't what she'd meant—and he knew it! Momentarily Gemma's jaw tightened as somewhere in the pit of her stomach she felt a knife thrust of pain. Stealing a man's heart, indeed! She doubted if she'd even borrowed Thor's. All *he* had given her was the doubtful benefit of his virile body—and even that had only been lent! She choked back the wave of bitterness that engulfed her. She might have been a woman scorned, but she wouldn't display her fury before his keen-eyed perception. Besides—she didn't hate him. Life would be much simpler at that moment if she had, and his remark had presumably been meant as a pleasantry, although it had touched her on the raw.

She forced herself to relax, stretching out her denim-clad legs, turning her face towards the sun's caress, her lips parting in soft laughter. 'I should hope I've changed—I was just seventeen when we first met, drunk with the joy of finally having left my schooldays behind me, intending to enjoy the summer holiday of a lifetime before applying myself to the serious task of finding a job.' She turned her head slightly to regard Thor through her lowered lashes. 'And if you must quote Shakespeare to me—get it right. It was outrageous fortune that the slings and arrows belonged to!'

'And did you enjoy the holiday, Gemma?' Quickly, he homed into the vulnerable heart of her confession, ignoring her pedantry.

She closed her eyes, feeling the heated caress of the sun touch her eyelids like a poultice. Those weeks with Thor had been Paradise, changing her whole outlook on life. At one point she had been eagerly contemplating a job where she could use her flair for modern languages, allied perhaps to the secretarial skills which she had learned in her final year. Yet only weeks later her ambitions had changed with the prospect of returning to Australia with Thor as his wife.

Her descent from Paradise to Purgatory without even a breathing space in Limbo had been accomplished with such brutality that it had been days after his sudden departure before she'd been able to find partial relief in tears, and longer still before she'd been able to take up the threads of her life again with any degree of purpose. None of which he should ever learn from her lips.

'It was fun,' she said now, pleased with the casual note that lent her voice a lazy drawl. 'Just the sort of interlude I needed—a fantasy to bridge the gap between childhood and adulthood. As a matter of fact, I'll always be grateful to you, Thor...' She paused, aware of his guarded scrutiny. 'You made me realise there was more to life than a regular job, a steady marriage. You opened up my horizons. If it hadn't been for your sudden departure I would never have thrown my fortune in with Laura and Noel. The last five years have been marvellous for me—one perpetual holiday in the sunshine...'

She deliberately made it sound sybaritic rather than the tough, time-consuming work it had been in reality. All she had to do now was make her final point and pray Thor would stop trying to reawaken memories which were better forgotten!

'Added to which, if it hadn't been for you, I would never have met Noel and fallen in love with him—so you see I have to thank you for preventing me from making a bad mistake.'

'But then I always did have your best interests at heart, Gemma—although it may not have been obvious to you at the time!' The bitterness in his rough retort surprised her, as unexpectedly his hand moved to cover her own.

From someone who'd made the unilateral decision to abort their planned wedding, it was hardly a credible statement!

'Well, then, you must be satisfied the way things have turned out!' She watched the long, thin scar over his eyebrow twitch, the only movement on his intense face until he spoke again.

'If you're happy—then I must be,' he agreed crisply.

So it *was* his conscience troubling him. Gemma sighed softly. Of course, hadn't he seen her father again? She doubted Robin Carson would have left the husky Australian in any doubt whatsoever as to how much she'd wept and wailed in the wake of his departure. Sometimes paternal love could be overpowering, especially when it was consciously compensating for past injustices—and in this case embarrassing!

Carefully she eased her imprisoned hand away. 'I *am* happy, Thor.' It wasn't a bad lie. In fact, it wasn't a lie at all in the sense that happy also meant content as apart from being deliriously head-over-heels in love, and she managed to smile softly into his blue stare to confirm her claim.

'And what about you, Thor? Have you had as much success with your personal life as your business one? Do you have some long-legged Brisbane blonde stacked away in the Outback, barbecueing kangaroo steaks for your batch of offspring?' It was Gemma's turn to cross-examine, and she managed it without a tremor in her voice, lifting one perfectly arched eyebrow in innocent enquiry.

'I'm not married, Gemma.' He lifted his coffee-cup to his mouth, firm tanned fingers sharply contrasting with the white china. Fingers that had stroked her body with a lover's tenderness... Angrily, Gemma thrust the thought away as he lowered the cup. 'There have been girlfriends, of course, but no one I ever wanted to marry.'

A small vein throbbed at his temple, as if it was important she believed him.

And of course, she did! Thor McCabe wasn't the faithful, marrying kind, but he was no woman-hater! His carnal appetite had been too developed, too perfected for him to embrace celibacy. She only hoped that these days he kept his attentions for the sophisticated type of woman who enjoyed playing love-games, and realised that the ardent lover's vows he swore were only passwords to deeper pleasures, with no real meaning of their own to justify them.

Finishing her coffee with a determined flourish, she decided to steer the conversation away from Thor's amorous exploits, enquiring abruptly, 'What did you say you did for a living when you first went back to Australia?' as she put the cup down. Since the day stretched ahead of them, it was important for Noel's sake she tried to regain their earlier sense of camaraderie.

For a moment she thought he wasn't going to answer. 'Gemma...' He started to speak, then seemed to change his mind before sighing resignedly. 'I used to round up cattle—mostly for branding and counting, sometimes for slaughter.'

'Oh, that's a shame!' She stared at his set face.

'You always were tender-hearted.' He gave her a crooked smile. 'No stray dog or starving cat was spared your attentions, I seem to remember.' The blue eyes softened as they dwelt on her upturned face. 'Once I recall having to stop the car so you could give artificial respiration to a bird which had struck the windscreen...'

'A finch!' She remembered it too, remembered holding the seemingly lifeless little creature in the palm of one hand while she'd massaged the downy breast. Unbelievably, against the odds, it had recovered in seconds and she'd sent it winging on its way, her eyes shining with happiness at its escape.

'Was it?' Thor's lips twisted wryly. 'Whatever it was, it was only one of the lame ducks you befriended while I was with you in England.'

'I was a country girl.' She shrugged her shoulders. 'It came naturally to me to care for creatures less fortunate than myself.'

'Only sometimes the old saying's right. It's necessary to be cruel to be kind. Life isn't always a better alternative than death, Gemma, and it's sentimental to believe it is.' She was shocked by the hard note that deepened his voice. He rose to his feet, ending the subject with final brusqueness. 'Do you have any further plans for today?'

Gemma watched while he paid the bill, her mind in a turmoil. So much of Thor McCabe was a mystery to her. Yet once she would have laid down her life for him. How ironic that her handsome Australian lover had chosen a herd of cattle instead of her.

'Gemma...' Thor grasped her arm with powerful fingers as she moved away from the table. 'Neither of us is the same person he or she was five years ago. Is it too much to ask you to try to regard me as a new acquaintance who might even become a friend, hmm?' His light eyes met her own in arrogant challenge. 'Or is your dislike of me so intense you'd prefer to call off this sightseeing tour altogether?'

'I'm quite prepared to show you around on the basis we agreed,' the words fell stiffly from Gemma's lips as she looked down her nose at the predatory fingers encircling her forearm, resenting the warm curl of remembered loving his touch invoked. 'And my feeling towards you is indifference rather than dislike.'

Since her true feelings defied description, it was the best she could do at short notice, but would he accept her graceless statement, or take her lack of enthusiasm as an excuse to call the whole thing off? A pang of guilt prodded her conscience. Noel was depending on her!

For a long second Thor's brilliant eyes held her own, as if he were about to denounce her as the liar she knew herself to be, before he removed the offending fingers from her body. 'OK, Gemma...' He surveyed her through narrowed eyelids. 'If that's the way you want it, it's fine by me. At least indifference is better than hostility, so for the time being I'll settle for it.' He paused slightly before sharpening his voice to a businesslike clarity. 'Where to now?'

Gemma had decided to have lunch in Fornells. During the hour or so's drive down one of the prettiest roads on the island, she leaned back in the passenger seat of Thor's rented Seat, closing her eyes and feigning sleep, allowing her mind to roam untrammelled through the past, where she'd learned the hard way about man's false promises and infidelity. She couldn't say the experience had turned her into a man-hater—but it had certainly shaken her confidence in the male sex. Never again would she want to live through a period of mourning similar to that she had undergone after his sudden decision to return to Australia without her.

At first, on the dreadful day he'd broken the news of his plans to her, she'd thought he'd been joking, then when it became clear he was telling her the truth, she'd stared at his one-way flight ticket, too shocked and honest to attempt to preserve her pride. 'But you'll be coming back?' she'd begged him to affirm it.

'No, Gemma.' He'd been pale and tense, but determined, and she'd shivered, sensing disaster.

'But I can come out to you?' her tear-filled eyes had begged him. 'When you've done whatever you're going back to do, then I can come, can't I?'

'No.' He'd quashed her hopes remorselessly. 'Don't you understand? I don't want you, Gemma. I don't want to marry you. What we shared was just a physical thing, infatuation, a midsummer madness, call it what you will.

It was enjoyable while it lasted, but it had no substance. I don't want to be tied down to domesticity, raising a family... I want to live the rest of my life free to go where I please, do what I want... It's over between us. I want you to forget about me...there's no future for us together, ever...'

If she'd been more worldlywise, less immersed in her own selfish activities—more interested in what was going on around her rather than in scouring pattern books for a wedding dress and looking for caterers in the local press, she would have seen it coming. In retrospect, all the clues had been there: Thor's odd silences, the occasional, bad-tempered frowns, the terse reply to a simple question. The unexplained phone calls and visits to London, shrugged off as visiting expatriates in Earl's Court. The summer idyll had already been dying, the call back to the wild a trumpet blast in his ears, long before he'd accepted the challenge to chase cattle!

If she'd been more knowledgeable, less tunnel-visioned, she would have realised that a man as physical as Thor—a man who loved the excitement and thrills of playing Australian Rules Football in the winter, who exulted in the speed and danger of power-boat racing in the summer—was too dynamic to handicap himself with the burden of a wife... Now, five years later, when she was well on the way to banishing the last lingering memories of him, his wandering feet had brought him back into her life. And he had the temerity to claim her friendship!

'I don't want you, Gemma.' That had been his very phrase, burned deep into her heart. Yet when he'd kissed her in Tramontana she'd known that to be a lie. Thor did still want her. What he didn't want, had never wanted, was commitment!

Despite the pain he'd caused her, she knew that the magnetism between them was as strong as ever, and that

Thor sensed it too. If ever she let down her defences he
would overcome her scruples, take everything she offered and leave her destitute. It had happened before—
it must never happen again!

'Right, this is it.' She opened her eyes as they entered
Fornells. 'If you park here we can walk across the road
to the restaurant. I hope you like lobster, because I
phoned up in advance and ordered us one each.'

'Lady, I love it!' He parked the car, walked round and
helped her out with an old-fashioned courtesy.

The lobster with its accompanying salad proved delicious, the crusty white bread fresh and tasty, and the
remnants of it much appreciated by the shoals of fish
that swam in the shallow sea at the edge of the open-air
restaurant, so used to human attention that they fed from
their hands.

It was mid-afternoon by the time they'd finished their
coffee and brandy, and Gemma suggested Thor might
like to look around the artists' colony. The narrow streets
were crowded with tourists, but the work so interesting
and varied that it was a pleasure to take one's time.

'What do you think of this one?' Thor indicated a
seascape, about eighteen inches square, the beauty of
which lay in its utter simplicity and clarity of colour. It
consisted only of sea, sky and a solitary small fishing-
boat seemingly suspended between the two, with the
figure of a man bending over in the boat, pulling in his
nets.

'It's lovely,' Gemma gave him her honest assessment.
The artist had captured the translucent colour of the sea
round the shallow harbour of Fornells—a curious
glistening shade that was neither blue nor turquoise nor
white, but an inspired mixture of all three. 'It gives an
impression of timelessness and total peace,' she qualified her opinion.

'You really like it, then?' He held the painting at arm's length, squinting at it through shuttered eyes.

'Definitely.' Gemma nodded her head vigorously. 'If you're looking for a souvenir of Menorca, I'm sure you'd never regret buying it.'

'The lady likes it . . .' Thor beckoned the artist towards them. 'I'll take it. How much?'

Not attempting to bargain on the price, he paid what was asked, commenting as his purchase was carefully wrapped, 'At least we still have some tastes in common.'

'Lobsters and oil colours,' she agreed demurely.

He shot her a quick glance. 'And who knows how many more we might discover before the day's over—or is it already ended?'

'That depends on you. Are you up to driving a fair way?'

'You're looking at a man who's used to driving two hundred miles for a game of cards.' He grinned at her—an uncomplicated twist of his lips which found an answering smile, recalling as it did the carefree Thor of her youth rather than the taciturn companion of the morning.

'OK, then. I'll take you to one of Menorca's most magnificent natural phenomena. I'll tell you more about it when we get there.'

'Well, what do you think of it?' Standing on a railed platform some sixty metres above an ultramarine sea which churned threateningly against the sheer cliff base that dropped beneath their precarious perch, Gemma posed the question.

'Awe-inspiring.' Thor turned his gaze from the vast stretch of sea to look back at the caves from which they'd just emerged—a vast natural honeycomb, the roof of which, in the main chamber, dipped as low as six feet

before soaring to arches which would have graced a
cathedral.

'Yes, it is impressive.' Gemma followed his gaze where
large openings along the length of the cliff allowed
natural light to pour into the chambers, illuminating
them with sunshine. 'No one knows how extensive they
are. As you probably noticed, many of the passages are
roped off. They're either too narrow or too dangerous
for exploration. But the main chamber has been used as
a disco at night time.'

She watched Thor as he wandered over to the edge of
the platform, resting one hand on the flimsy rustic barrier
as he gazed down at a sailing yacht anchored a little distance from the base of the rock, her white topsail startling against the navy depths of the deep waters. She
quelled an instinct to exhort him to be careful, reminding herself that she no longer had any rights over
his behaviour, particularly not the ones that followed in
the wake of loving and being loved.

'You said something about a legend when we were
inside?' He turned from his contemplation of the calm
scene, genuine interest mirrored on his face. 'Something
to do with this guy Xuroy who gave his name to the
place?'

'That's right.' Gemma nodded her dark head. 'Over
a hundred years before the birth of Christ, Xuroy was
a galley slave who escaped when his ship was off the
coast. He found sanctuary in these caves through some
secret entrance, and lived here hunting for food and living
off the land. One day he met the daughter of one of the
Roman governors of the island. It was love at first sight,
and he captured her and brought her back with him.'
She sighed. 'He must have been a remarkable young
man, or else she was tired of the effete style of life the
Romans enjoyed, for it seems she returned his love and
willingly gave up everything to share his exile.'

'A remarkable young man, indeed.' Thor took advantage of her pause for breath to comment with a gentle, mocking smile. 'Do I take it their married life was idyllic?'

'For a while.' Gemma nodded. 'Despite all the hazards surrounding them, and Xuroy's constant fear of capture and death, they thrived and she bore him two sons. Then their luck changed. One bitter winter's night, something happened that had never been known to happen before. It snowed. Poor Xuroy, stumbling back against the bitter wind, anxious to regain the safety of his cave and the loving arms of his family, never realised his footprints lay indented in the snow.'

'So the Romans found him?'

'The following morning. Rather than face death at their merciless hands he jumped from the opening into the sea and was killed instantly as his body hit the rocks.'

'A tragic ending,' Thor mused. 'What happened to the girl?'

'The legend says she took one look at the Roman soldiers, their hands held out in friendship to return her to her grieving father—then she took her sons by each hand and followed the man she loved to eternity.'

'Very touching—especially the way you told it.' Again Gemma was subjected to a brilliant, mocking smile. So she was a romantic at heart? It was something she wasn't going to apologise for! 'You know, Gemma,' he continued confidingly, coming towards her and flinging a casual arm round her shoulders, 'I could just picture the blond Xuroy with his blue eyes and his Roman lady with her dark eyes and nut-brown hair, and their children— one fair like him, the other dark like his mother...'

On the point of protesting that she hadn't mentioned anything about colouring, Gemma hesitated. Thor's imagination wasn't far from the mark. Xuroy's nationality wasn't known, but it was assumed he'd come from some northern capital conquered by the Romans at the time and was most probably Anglo-Saxon. As for the governor's daughter, it didn't take a lot of intelligence to guess she had a Latin cast of feature.

'Yes, I saw it all quite plainly.' Thor's voice seemed suddenly husky as he lifted a hand to touch the silky fringe of hair that brushed her forehead. 'The girl looked just like you.'

Gemma drew in a trembling breath, uncertain how to react to this unexpected moment of intimacy. But she mustn't let him see how easily his little games could disturb her. She must learn to refer to their past friendship as if it meant as little to her as it had to him.

'And doubtless you cast yourself in the heroic role of Xuroy?' she spoke flippantly, only too painfully aware that that was exactly what *she'd* done. In her mind, Xuroy who'd stood poised on the cliff edge before hurtling to certain death had had the same grace, the lithe body, the smooth, developed muscles of the man beside her. The man who'd invited her to his villa and welcomed her wearing only brief bathing shorts.

In a kind of despair she realised that, despite what she consciously felt about Thor McCabe, deep in her subconscious mind she'd preserved his image—not as the inconsiderate, fickle buccaneer he undoubtedly was, but as the tender, gentle lover he'd once been! If nothing else good came of their brief reunion, she must use this opportunity to weed him out of her heart and her life for ever!

'Of course,' he acknowledged her supposition silkily. 'We still make a very attractive pair.'

'A thought that Noel would find as unamusing as I do!' She moved sharply away from him. 'It's time we were leaving!'

'Does he know we were lovers? Does he, Gemma?' He was close behind her on the long sweep of steep steps cut into the cliffs, as she ignored the question, increasing the rate of her ascent.

'Answer me, damn you!' She was no match for Thor's long stride. Catching her round the waist, he pressed her back against the uneven cliff face. 'He must have known you were no virgin,' he went on stubbornly. 'But does he know I was the first man in your life? Does he?' He glared down at her.

A wild spurt of anger rose inside her. Anyone would think he was accusing her of being unfaithful with Noel! Dear God, how she'd love to take a swipe at the pugnacious jaw, wipe that angry look of superiority from his stern countenance. Teeth gritted, she counted to ten very slowly. Dignity. She must keep her dignity.

'Yes, he knows.' She spoke with icy deliberation. 'Though you've no right to ask me such a question. I've no secrets from Noel. He's the kindest, most understanding, most compassionate man I've ever known. Any girl would be proud to marry him.' She held his light blue gaze with steady regard. 'It didn't take me long to realise that you and I had nothing in common, Thor. You were eight years older, from the other side of the world, raised in wide open spaces... It would have been disaster. The fact is, you realised the truth before I did, that's all. Noel is totally different. We started as friends and over the years our relationship changed, deepened...'

'You don't love him as you used to love me!' It was a low, vibrant accusation, and Gemma reacted to it as if she'd been stung.

'No, I don't!' Her eyes sparkled with an inner fury. 'I was an inexperienced adolescent when I met you, and I loved you with a childlike faith. Well, knowing you made me grow up. I'm a better judge of men now than I ever was and, let me tell you, Noel is worth twice as much as you any day!' She made a deprecating twist of her lips. 'Oh, not necessarily materially, I grant you.

But where it counts—here!' At last she'd managed to
dislodge his hold, and slammed her fist against her own
heart to illustrate her point.

She was close to tears, breathing heavily, almost convinced that she *was* in love with Noel, engaged to marry
him. She only hoped she'd at last convinced Thor of the
same thing. What did he think he was achieving, anyway?
He'd never loved her, so it wasn't jealousy. It had to be
a primitive male instinct that resented another male
poaching what had once been his preserves. In view of
his earlier assertion that he was glad she was happy, it
was an attitude she resented with every fibre of her being!

He was staring down at her, his face strained, his lips
parted, his chest heaving with more than the effort of
the climb. For one wild moment she imagined he was
about to lower his head and kiss her, not with tenderness
as he had in the past, but with a punitive intent she'd
done nothing to deserve. Then to her utter relief there
was the sound of voices behind them and the moment
passed.

Her throat achingly dry, she swallowed painfully.
'Now, shall we leave before that party of tourists catches
up with us?'

She started climbing the steps again as he nodded. Her
back was sore where the sharp edges of rock had pressed
into her tender flesh. But it was as nothing to the pain
in her heart. Damn Thor McCabe for looking like he
did, for being what he was, but most of all for coming
back into her life when she'd almost forgotten him and
re-awakening the past with such perseverance.

By the time they reached Mahón the long fingers of
the setting sun were burnishing the waters of the inlet,
the magnificent harbour that could hold all the navies
of the world at anchor in its three-and-a-half-mile sweep
to the sea.

They'd driven in silence, Gemma immersed in her own
thoughts, Thor, his profile hard and set, staring out at

the road ahead. She supposed she'd been a little harsh with him, her answers bordering on rudeness, but then he'd touched places that were still sore. Still, for Noel's sake, perhaps she should re-offer the hand of friendship.

'There's one more place I could show you,' she ventured softly. 'If you're interested.'

He turned towards her slightly, raising enquiring eyebrows.

'Have you heard of Golden Farm?'

'Surely,' he nodded. 'Nelson's house, isn't it?'

'That's right. It's on the far side of the inlet.' She pointed through the windscreen. 'If you take that road instead of turning down here you'll reach it in a few minutes. It's privately owned and not open to the public, but I know one of the gardeners. He'll let us go into the garden. The view of the harbour from there is breathtaking.'

'Why not?' He swung the steering wheel in the direction indicated.

The Farm hadn't been part of her original itinerary, but as they approached the gates to the house Gemma was glad she'd come. The beautiful small garden with its abundance of trees, small beds of flowers set into paving stones and two-hundred-year-old blue jasmine always had a soothing effect on her. Tonight it was particularly beautiful as the Mediterranean dusk passed quickly to darkness.

She stood at Thor's side, watching the lights of the tall hotels on the far bank spring into life, the golden illuminations of Mahón itself gleam against the velvet darkness of the sky. Positioned as they were on the high balustrade surrounding the garden, it was as if fairyland were opening up at their feet.

'Look...' Gemma touched Thor's arm lightly, drawing his attention to the dock, where a sudden displacement of light heralded the departure of the evening ferry to

Barcelona. As the golden wedge passed slowly beneath them on her journey towards the open sea, Gemma shivered.

Almost tentatively, Thor placed his arm round her shoulders. Before she realised what she was doing, Gemma moved instinctively closer to him. It was a mistake, and a bad one. Thor's animal warmth welcomed her cool skin as his hand drifted slowly on her upper arm. She wanted to be indifferent to him, but there was a quality in him that escaped her definition. Whatever its source, it had taken her indifference and begun to mould it into something dangerously like attraction.

Pulling herself together with an effort, she lifted her face towards him. 'Thor...'

She'd intended saying, 'Thor, we ought to leave now,' but she'd only spoken his name, and that one word had left her mouth parted and vulnerable.

He bent his head and kissed her. His action was so shockingly unexpected, it overcame all her powers of resistance. Even while her mind was telling her the absolute folly of returning his embrace, her mouth was enjoying him.

In that instant she was aware only of the beautiful strength of his body against hers, the physical compatibility that moulded them to a rapturous harmony.

'Gemma, Gemma—you're still as delicious as I remember...' His words trembled against her skin as his mouth scorched it, trailing its passionate lips in a hungry pursuit of her cheeks, her forehead, the sculpted line of her pretty chin.

Dazed by her own violent reactions, Gemma allowed herself the luxury, the sheer joy of running her fingers through his hair, brushing it back from his face, letting it spring back lop-sided across his forehead. In an agony of remembrance, she drifted her hands across his shoulders, caressing the gentle swell of the muscles. She allowed her hands to wander down his chest, feeling the fast trip of his heartbeat, hearing his laboured breathing, aware that his body was quickening in masculine appreciation and desire, but ignoring all the danger signals as she returned his greedy embrace.

She'd lived without him for so long, dreamed of holding him once more in her arms, needed to re-live the fantasy of perfect love. Perhaps in that instant that he'd kissed her she'd persuaded herself there'd be no damage done if she responded—just this once. She'd been wrong. Like an addict she'd craved what was forbidden and, having stolen a sweet portion, her hunger, far from being satiated, had grown worse.

With a little moan she tried to push Thor away, only to find he was no dream fantasy to be dismissed at will. His hands travelled over the firm curves of her hips with an experienced touch, rose to slide with practised ease beneath her T-shirt, capturing her breasts in their flimsy nylon covering.

If she'd ever doubted she was playing with fire, those doubts became ashes. Now she began to struggle frantically in his arms, using the palms of her hands against his stomach in an effort to dislodge his hold. Then, as this had little effect, she balled her hands into fists, knuckling them hard into his firm flesh, deliberately and cruelly rejecting him.

Reluctantly Thor released her, reaching out a hand to tip her chin so he could look down straight into the emptiness of her eyes.

'What's wrong, Gemma?' he asked quietly.

'Nothing,' she told him tersely. Only the fact that he appeared to think that because he'd once possessed her, it gave him the right to some kind of leasehold on her! 'We'd better be going now. Noel will be expecting me.'

'Why did you bring me here?' His tone was soft, almost menacing, but she thought she detected a slight shake in it which betrayed his arousal.

'It seemed a good way to end the evening. Not only is this place of historical interest, it's also very beautiful.' She tried to justify her decision, still uncertain of the reality of her motives herself.

'The perfect tour, hmm?' There was an odd smile playing round the corners of his mouth. 'Are you quite sure there wasn't an ulterior motive—like having a little fun behind Noel's back?' Beneath the calm, impersonal tone of his voice, Gemma detected a thread of anger and felt a qualm of unease.

'What happened just now was none of my doing!' she retorted furiously.

'No?' He made a grab for her upper arms, pinioning her and drawing her closer to him than she cared to be. 'With all the experience you've gained in the past five years, are you trying to tell me that you weren't offering an invitation with every movement of your delectable body?'

'Of course I wasn't!' She licked her dry lips fearfully. Not consciously she wasn't, but trust him to misunderstand! Wasn't this the man who had belittled everything she'd once felt for him by reducing her reaction to mere sexual chemistry?

A wave of colour flooded her face at his crude indictment, indetectable in the dim light, but accompanied by a surge of heat that made her cheeks burn.

'You never used to be a flirt, Gemma,' he accused her quietly. 'What did you want to do? Prove to yourself that you still have the power to arouse me?' He made a sound of disgust, pushing her away from him as if to touch her soiled him. 'Because, if that was it, you've got your answer, haven't you?'

Bereft for words, Gemma hung her head, staring down at her sandalled feet. 'Only, if the fancy takes you again, don't fool yourself you're still playing around with a considerate twenty-five-year-old! A lot of things have happened to me in the past five years, Gemma—I can never again be the man I once was. Now, if I'm offered something I want—I take it first, and ask the questions later!'

Had she led him on? No! Vehemently, she denied it to herself. His own imagination and male ego had betrayed him, and she was being made to take the blame. Well, she, too, had changed since she last set eyes on him. She was stronger, harder, more able to protect herself—physically and emotionally. And she had Noel's allegiance to sustain her! There was no way of denying her response to Thor—but she could belittle it...

She raised a negligent shoulder. 'What's a little flirtation anyway, Thor? We live in a liberal age. Noel knows I'm basically faithful to him.'

'I see.' His hand on her arm was rough as he turned her away from the panorama beneath them. 'In that case, we'd better not disappoint him.'

Listlessly, Gemma allowed herself to be guided back to the car to sit silently beside a grim-faced Thor, her mind a maze of tortured thoughts. She knew why he'd left her five years ago. At the time his explanation had been explicit and to the point. Now Parangas had brought him back to her side, but surely he couldn't believe she would fall into his lap again like the fabled ripe peach?

It was only when they were in sight of the farmhouse that Thor addressed her, his tone unemotional, as if the strange scene at Golden Farm had never happened. 'What are our plans for tomorrow, Gemma?'

'I have to be on duty at La Langousta from lunchtime onwards,' she answered honestly, following his lead in pleasantness. 'But the day after's rather special. It's the Feast of St. John, and there are some rather splendid celebrations in Ciudadela, the old Moorish capital the other side of the island.'

'That sounds like fun.' He was coolly impersonal.

'It generally is.' She smiled her agreement through stiff lips. 'It doesn't really start until the evening, so I wondered if you'd like to make an early start, spend the morning on one of the beaches and have lunch at a hotel en route.'

'Whatever you think's best.' He turned into the narrow road leading to the farmhouse, stopping the car several yards from the building. 'I want to thank you for a very enjoyable day.' Blue eyes regarded her steadily from beneath their fan of dark lashes.

'I enjoyed it too, Thor,' she said politely, opening the car door and swinging her legs to the ground. It was true. She had enjoyed being with him, every moment in his company a bonus, a bitter one for all that, and one she'd never admit to him. 'It's always a pleasure to show a stranger round the island. I'll look forward to seeing you again the day after tomorrow. We can arrange times on the phone.' She alighted from the car, closing the door behind her.

'Gemma, wait!' He reached behind him. 'Here. Take this with you. I bought it for you.'

'Oh, Thor!' She was gazing down at the parcel containing the painting he'd bought at Fornells. A large lump seemed to rise in her throat. 'But I can't...'

'Of course you can.' He gave her a dazzling smile which to her discerning gaze held no humour and very little friendship. 'Just regard it as an early wedding present for you and Noel.'

He put the car in gear and drove off, leaving her standing looking after him, the picture of the calm and peaceful harbour of Fornells clutched in her hands. It was a direct contrast to the darkness and storm she felt in her heart.

CHAPTER FOUR

'A VERY thoughtful gesture!' Noel surveyed the oil colour, with a marked lack of enthusiasm, over breakfast the following morning. 'I admire his taste, but I'm not so sure about the motives behind his generosity. What's he after, Gem?'

'I wish I knew.' She toyed with the croissant on her plate. 'I guess I just don't know the etiquette for dealing with old love affairs. It's not as if I was the one to walk out on him, but he seems to regard the fact that I'm engaged to you to be some kind of personal challenge to his New World *machismo*!'

'The fiction—not the fact . . .' Noel corrected her with a wry smile. 'Sounds like jealousy to me!'

'Hardly!' Gemma broke off a piece of the bread with impatient fingers. 'He was the one to call it a day! And five years, Noel! If he did have regrets after he left I wasn't on another planet, was I? He could always have reached me through Dad if he'd wanted to. No. My guess is it's just a way of amusing himself before he moves on again.' She shrugged her shoulders philosophically. 'I suppose I'm partly to blame. I did suggest that he'd been the first of many. In retrospect, that was a mistake. He's . . .' She hesitated as Noel frowned. 'He's changed a lot, Noel. When I knew him in England he was much easier to get along with. Now there's something about him I can't put my finger on—a kind of intensity, a suppressed anger that's never far from the surface . . .' She paused to take a mouthful of croissant, unwilling to admit aloud that she found the new Thor a little frightening.

'What exactly did go wrong between you?' Noel gazed at her sympathetically. 'Did you have some great bust-up—a lover's quarrel?'

'No, nothing like that.' She shook her head. 'If we had, what happened would have been much easier to understand. But one moment he was talking about getting married and going back to Australia...living somewhere along the Queensland coast. He was a qualified engineer with enough capital to buy a good property...' A bitter laugh escaped her lips. 'The next he was telling me he didn't want marriage after all, that our attraction had been purely physical and he didn't want to be tied down!'

'The bastard!' Noel interjected with feeling.

'That's what I thought at first,' Gemma concurred with a sigh, 'but afterwards I realised it would have been far worse if he'd been too afraid to go back on his word, and he'd embroiled me in a loveless marriage all those miles away from my old home.' She shrugged her shoulders. 'At least we hadn't actually named the day.'

'And now he's got the damned nerve to make a nuisance of himself again—as if he hasn't already done enough damage!' Noel rose to his feet with every sign of anger. 'Look, Gem, why don't we tell him to get lost?'

'Because we need his money,' she smiled at his angry face.

'Not if the interest we're asked to pay on it is your peace of mind.'

'Noel, darling, I appreciate what you're saying.' She left the table to go to him. 'But I want to go on with this.' She put a restraining hand on his arm as he started to make an angry retort. 'To be honest with you, Thor McCabe went out of my life with such—such speed, and the shock was so great, I never really had time to come completely to terms with losing him. If I could have grown to like him less, been more aware of his faults, I think it would have been easier. But I was totally infatuated with him, more like a worshipper at the shrine of a god than a flesh and blood woman who considered herself his equal.' She allowed herself a wry smile. 'What I'm trying to say is, now I have the opportunity of seeing his feet of clay, and I want to make the most of it. This way I may be able to rout him out of my system for once and for all.'

'And if he wants to become your lover again—can you handle it without becoming even more hurt?' Noel looked up into her clear, dark eyes. 'Because from where I'm sitting that's exactly what he intends!'

'You may be right.' After last night, how could she doubt Thor's desire for her? 'But he won't force himself on me...' She lowered troubled eyes to Noel's grim face. 'As long as I make it quite clear I intend to remain faithful to you, I can keep him in his place...' Her voice tailed off as Noel pounced on her indecision.

'What place is that, Gem? When you first asked me to help you out I thought it was because you hated the guy; now I'm beginning to believe the truth is you're still in love with him, and the protection you're asking for is against your own needs and desires!'

'No!' Anguish sharpened her retort. 'How could I be, Noel? I'd have to be totally without self-respect to nurture any feeling for a man who used me when I was too young and experienced to realise what he was doing.'

'Not necessarily, Gem.' He looked at her with amused tolerance. 'The human heart isn't logical. And if your heart and your head are telling you different things, then it's up to you to choose which one to follow. Only—be careful.'

'I don't love Thor McCabe, and I certainly don't want to have an affair with him!' Stubbornly Gemma made her point, inviting Noel's dissent with a flash of her dark eyes. 'Do I take it you no longer want to act the part of my fiancé?'

'Don't be silly, Gem. You know I'll stand by you.' He gave her arm a reassuring squeeze before returning his attention to his breakfast. 'As long as you don't expect me to go actually as far as the altar!'

Despite the firm assurance she'd given Noel, Gemma experienced a few qualms as she walked along the waterfront a little later, enjoying the early morning solitude. She'd been shocked to discover just how much she could still respond to Thor. Thank heavens she had a day to herself, to gird together her ragged defences, before she had to see him again!

When the market opened she wandered up the steps from the port towards the Plaza del Carmen, entering the cool, white, cloistered building with a sense of pleasure. Shopping for food never ceased to give her satisfaction here, where red and green peppers, purple aubergines, peaches and cherries were set off to perfection against the white walls and arches, and where butcher's shops well stocked with veal and pork, ducks and partridge, and where stalls with canned foods imported from all over the world offered a gourmet choice. Not to mention the large range of cheeses and continental sausages of all descriptions that were available. She browsed around, purchasing a few items to keep the kitchen at the farmhouse well stocked, before strolling towards the square by the fountain and ordering a coffee.

Inevitably her thoughts returned to the previous day and her companion. Was she being stupid in agreeing to see Thor again like this? She had to admit that her body could still thrill to his touch, but that wasn't love. Love couldn't exist without trust, and Thor had killed off every last atom of that the day he'd abandoned her so cruelly.

It was midday when she reached La Langousta, walking through one of the white-painted Moorish arches into its cool courtyard, built round a small fountain. Bench seats upholstered in cool, dark blue fabric contrasted with the white walls; low, wooden tables bore vases of fresh flowers. On the ledges of the arched open windows overlooking the harbour were pots of geraniums and small cacti, while on the floor larger terracotta pots were grouped, overspilling with flowers and foliage.

Gemma cast a practised eye round the open-air patio with its large sun umbrellas offering a welcome shade, and found nothing to fault. The whole restaurant had been designed to replicate a corner of Andalucia. It might not be an original idea, but it had been well carried out, and the effect was extremely attractive.

With so many hotels only offering an evening meal, La Langousta had a good luncheon trade. Since the early menu was kept simple and scarcely varied from day to day, Noel employed only two other girls beside herself to cope with it.

Walking through into the kitchens expecting to find Margarita and Rosa, she stopped in surprise as Josephina looked up from her task of preparing salads to greet her.

'You haven't heard, then?' the Spanish girl read Gemma's amazement.

'Heard what? I left home early this morning.'

'Rosa's in the infirmary. She may have appendicitis. So Noel has asked me if I can take her place here and at Tramontana until further notice.'

'Poor Rosa!' Gemma sympathised with genuine feeling. 'But what about your other jobs, Josephina?' The tips she must receive from her wealthy clients at the villas would far outweigh what would be an economic salary for Noel to pay her—especially now!

'They're not important!' Josephina shrugged her shoulders as she continued with her preparations. 'Only Mr McCabe. I promised I'd cook for him if he entertains at the Villa Sabina, and Noel says I must keep my word to him.'

'Of course,' Gemma commented drily. In view of what *she* was prepared to do to ingratiate herself with the enigmatic Australian, it would hardly behove Noel to interfere with Thor's domestic arrangements. And, as far as Josephina's agreement to help out was concerned, she guessed that was based more on a feeling of gratitude towards Noel for the encouragement and work he gave her young brother, than for mere mercenary reasons.

'Can you and Margarita cope by yourselves tomorrow?' she asked anxiously, suddenly recalling her offer to Thor.

'Of course!' the Spanish girl responded instantly. 'If it gets very busy at Tramontana in the evening, then Leo will have to work a little harder and play a little less!'

It was only much later in the afternoon, as the two girls cleared away the last of the plates, that Gemma asked Josephina a question that had been intriguing her.

'Does Mr McCabe expect to do much entertaining, do you know?'

The Spanish girl was only too eager to display her knowledge. 'He did tell me an Australian friend of his is cruising in the Mediterranean and he hopes to persuade him to drop anchor in Mahón, and that if he does he'd like to lay on something special,' she volunteered.

So Thor McCabe was expecting visitors, was he? Perhaps when they arrived he'd leave her, Gemma, in peace. Tomorrow might well be the last day she'd spend any real length of time in his company. That being so,

perhaps she could afford to relax a little. She pursed her
pretty mouth thoughtfully as she slowly removed the
apron she'd worn to protect her pale cotton dress.

Tomorrow she'd make quite sure Thor McCabe had
something to remember about Menorca.

The sound of the phone bleeping at the precise moment
she stepped out of the shower the following morning set
Gemma's heart racing as she quickly placed a towel
sarong-style under her arms, tucking in the free end to
hold it in place.

Picking up the phone in one hand, she used the other
to pat herself dry as she announced her number into the
mouthpiece.

'Everything set as originally planned?' It was Thor as
she'd half expected, the pleasant timbre of his voice
seemingly enhanced by the telephone. A tiny shiver
trembled across her bare skin as the warm tones reached
out caressingly.

Her fingers tightened round the receiver as she tried
to keep her voice impersonal. 'Yes, sure. Unless you want
to do something different? It occurred to me that the
beach might not have much attraction for you after your
South Sea Island!'

'Coral Sea Island.' She heard the amusement in his
voice as he corrected her. 'And I can assure you I'm not
old enough to find any of my appetites jaded. Besides,
I have to judge what attracts tourists here and, more
important, brings them back again. Beaches must be
pretty high on that list, don't you think? We mustn't
forget the whole purpose of this exercise, must we?'

Gemma would have felt a lot happier if she'd been
convinced the whole purpose of the exercise was what
she'd been told! But she wasn't about to confide her
doubts on that matter. 'Well, the beach I have in mind
isn't one of the more popular ones,' she told him, a trifle

tartly. 'I thought I'd take you off the beaten track, show you that there are still empty beaches here in the height of summer, if you know where to look.'

'Sounds something right after my own heart.' The lazy Australian drawl purred across the wire.

'Well, let's hope so!' she observed briskly, adding as an afterthought, 'I'd better warn you in advance: it's very primitive. There aren't any changing facilities, no bars, not even any shade. Anything you want you have to take with you.'

'That's precisely what I shall be doing.' The retort was so swift, it took Gemma off guard. Warm blood rose to her face as the implication in Thor's comment penetrated her consciousness. There had been no mistaking the warm suggestiveness of his reaction. Her teeth gritted in annoyance. So it was OK for Thor McCabe to flirt with her—provided she'd didn't reciprocate!

It was while she was trying to regain her composure that Noel chose to walk down the stairs towards her, clad in a towelling bathrobe and yawning widely.

'Who's on the phone, darling?' Approaching her closely, to her utter astonishment he planted a noisy kiss on her bare shoulder, continuing to speak as she regarded him with silent consternation. 'I wish you'd put some clothes on before you answer the phone.' He grinned at her, his lips close enough to the mouthpiece for his words to travel down the line. 'Or are you coming back to bed again, hmm?' Again he pressed a noisy salutation on her shoulder.

'Noel!' It was so unlike him to fool around like this, and so early in the morning too, when he was usually half-asleep, that she was torn between irritation and surprise. 'This is important!' She pushed him away, her eyes daring him to come nearer as she spoke anxiously into the phone.

'Thor? Are you still there?' With an effort, she collected her disordered thoughts. 'I'm sorry, that was Noel playing around.'

'Well, that's a relief,' was the dry rejoinder. 'I thought for a moment you were running a disorderly house. Do I take it we'll be making a late start?'

Resolutely she ignored the implication behind his question. 'I'll be ready to leave in an hour,' she responded crisply, pleased she was able to keep her tone so businesslike. 'The best thing will be to dress for the beach and take a change of clothes for the afternoon. If we stop off for lunch at one of the big hotels along the coast we can use their facilities to shower and change.'

'An hour, then.' Gemma's ear reacted painfully to the noise of Thor's receiver being replaced with unnecessary firmness.

'Ouch!' She rubbed the injured organ reflectively, her dark eyes accusing as they accosted Noel. 'What was all that in aid of?' she enquired tautly. 'That was Thor McCabe I was speaking to.'

'Who else?' Noel regarded her icy expression askance. 'What's wrong, Gem? I thought you wanted him to believe you and I were engaged to be married?'

'Yes, I did!' She couldn't deny it, and why would she want to? A stable relationship was the greatest barrier she could erect against the Australian's pernicious charm. 'I just didn't want our relationship to appear too blatant.' She looked away, unable to meet his eyes as she wrested with her own emotions.

'Blatant!' Noel sounded as if he couldn't believe what he'd heard. 'Dear God, Gem, the man knows we're sharing the same house, he believes we're going to get married, he knows damn well you're no virgin... Are you trying to tell me you expect him to think we're living in celibacy?'

Put like that, her objections did sound ridiculous. Of course Thor McCabe believed she slept with Noel. Gemma bit her lip ruefully, surprised at the unexpected vehemence of Noel's tone. Was it because he believed she'd cast an indirect slur on his masculinity? she wondered.

Just because there had been no sexual spark between her and Laura's brother, it didn't mean Noel wasn't attractive to and attracted by the opposite sex in general. To date, his liaisons had been of brief duration, their length preordained by the duration of a holiday, but there was no doubt in her mind that Noel would eventually find the girl of his dreams, settle down and make a loving husband.

He was so different from Thor, but none the less a virile man for all that. It had been selfish of her to ask him to play a major role in her own life and then try to relegate it, especially as Thor and Noel were involved in business. Thor had been her lover. In his assumed role, Noel would expect to portray a similar relationship, if only to boost his own ego and meet the other man as an equal.

'No, of course not,' she answered his question sheepishly. 'I'm sorry, Noel. It's just that you took me a bit by surprise. But you're quite right. It's in all our interests for Thor McCabe to believe you and I are deeply committed to each other.' Especially after yesterday, she added silently to herself.

How could she explain to anyone the intensity of the emotions Thor had aroused in her all those years ago? Hero-worship, love, fear and the ultimate, mortifying shock as she'd been forced to realise that the attractive physique, the mental agility, the bright intelligence and friendly charm had hidden a vacillating spirit?

The former qualities could so easily attract her again—but the awareness of his inner indecision would never

be erased from her mind. Thor had been under no
pressure to offer her marriage. She'd loved him so completely, she'd never put a price on her body. He'd chosen
willingly to show her a sight of Paradise, then slammed
the gates in her face. There had been no gentleness or
compassion in his rejection. It had been abrupt and cruel,
leaving her to search her own personality for the flaw
that had alienated him so utterly.

She uttered a sigh of exasperation. This was getting
her nowhere. If she didn't intend to keep Thor waiting,
she'd have to get a move on.

The hired Seat arrived an hour later, almost to the
minute, its occupant emerging to display the long,
smoothly muscled legs with their bronze tan that Gemma
recalled so well from their earlier meeting at the Villa
Sabina. Brief navy shorts fitted his lean hips, topped by
a navy and white striped cotton T-shirt that clung lovingly
to his well-developed pectorals. At the sight of him a
sharp pang of loss scythed through her, its impact so
great that she stopped momentarily in her tracks. This
was absurd! How could she survive a day in his company
if she was trembling after the first moment?

'Anything wrong?' He'd opened the passenger door
for her and was standing back, a faint smile on his lips
as his eyes passed in quick assessment over her. White
cotton shorts added a modest cover to the scarlet bikini
briefs beneath them, while she'd covered the top with a
matching scarlet cotton blouse, sleeves rolled up, neck
unbuttoned, ends tied neatly around her midriff, dis-
playing just a couple of inches of honey-gold skin before
the waistband of her shorts. It was eminently suitable
for a trip to the beach, but now, with Thor's eyes resting
speculatively on her, she felt a good deal more exposed
than she was.

'No—I——' Unable to meet the sheer masculine admiration she'd read briefly in his gaze, she dropped her

eyes, allowing them to fall on the long stretch of his naked legs, their surface lightly flecked with hair that gleamed a dull gold. Instantly she received inspiration. 'I just remembered, I should have warned you to wear shoes with a thick sole. It's a bit of a walk over rough ground to the beach I have in mind.' She nodded approvingly at the tough-soled sandals he lifted obediently for her inspection. 'They're fine.'

'He could always have borrowed mine.' Noel walked out from the farmhouse, flinging a proprietorial arm round her shoulders. Penitent for her earlier ingratitude, she leant against him, accepting the embrace. His fingers moved easily on her shoulders, but it was Thor he addressed. 'Chap in Mercadel makes sandals out of cowhide and rubber tyres—guaranteed for five thousand miles.'

'Really? I'll remember that if I ever get an ambition to walk round the world. In the meantime, I guess I can manage with what I've got. I don't imagine the going will be all that tough.'

'I wouldn't depend on that!' Noel's eyes gleamed with laughter as he squeezed Gemma's arm affectionately. 'My wife-to-be's a very tough lady, when she gets the bit between her teeth. She might surprise you yet!'

'I doubt it,' Thor observed drily, motioning her to get into the car. 'Gemma and I are old friends. There's not a great deal about her I don't already know.'

'On the contrary, McCabe—I'd say you hardly know her at all!' Noel's smile died from his eyes. 'And that's the way I want it kept!'

'My dear Shelton . . .' Thor's calm reply had overtones of irony as he raised his dark eyebrows in astonishment. 'I can assure you she'll come to no harm in my company. I don't take advantage of unwilling ladies, if that's what you're insinuating—and since Gemma is determined to marry you it follows she *would* be unwilling, doesn't it?'

His white teeth showed in a fleeting, humourless smile as he took the carrier bag in which she'd packed a change of clothes from her hand and placed it carefully on the back seat, before setting the car into gear and moving smoothly away, leaving Noel staring after them.

'Where to, Gemma?'

'Take the road to Es Grau.' She indicated the position on the map he offered her. 'I'll tell you when to stop.' She was still fuming from his nonchalant exchange with Noel, and her annoyance showed in the coldness of her voice.

Thor slanted her an amused look. 'Cross because I tweaked your pussycat's tail?'

'What you said was uncalled for. Noel knows he doesn't have any cause to be jealous of me—and he's no pussycat. You can't go around judging everyone by your own standards.'

'Oh, but I don't, sweetheart! Just the men.'

'Noel's more of a man than you'll ever be!' she flung back instantly. 'There's more to masculinity than muscles. Noel may not have your build, or your charisma, but then he lacks your ruthlessness and insincerity, and that makes him twice the man in my book!'

'I'm glad you think so!' But he didn't look particularly pleased as his fingers tightened on the wheel. 'But in my experience it's not always the meek who inherit the earth. Sometimes in this life a man has to fight pretty damned hard for the things he really wants, and sometimes the rules get a bit bent!'

'And you think Noel wouldn't fight?' she asked icily.

'That's what I mean to find out.' He swore softly as the car bumped through a series of ruts.

'It's Parangas, isn't it?' She forced herself to keep calm. 'You're going to stipulate some outlandish conditions to your offer!' Her heart plummeted as she envisaged Noel's disappointment. He had so little leeway in which to operate.

'What offer, Gemma?' His stern profile offered her nothing. 'I wasn't aware I'd even made an offer yet.'

Anger choked in her throat. 'Then there's no point in continuing this tour. You'd better take me back to San Luis straight away.'

'So you can go back to bed with Noel?' His mouth twisted disparagingly. 'No, I don't think that's a good idea. Besides, I haven't made up my mind yet, and I've been looking forward to our being together for a whole day. There's still a possibility I might decide in your favour.'

'Is there?' She made no attempt to hide her disbelief. 'You've made it quite clear that you don't like Noel, and I doubt you've added philanthropy to your many virtues!' Scorn sharpened her voice, and she was surprised to see Thor's lips twitch with suppressed laughter.

'At least you do credit me with some virtues, then, Gemma? I was beginning to believe from the black looks you've been giving me these last days that my personal credit rating with you was nil.'

Damn his arrogance! Gemma made a point of staring out of the window, her lips firmly clamped. She sensed rather than heard his exasperated sigh.

'So my first impressions of your lover are that he's irresolute. A man who finds it difficult to take a decision and stick with it.' If he heard her swift, indrawn hiss of breath at his duplicity, he ignored it, continuing smoothly. 'His personal life is none of my business, but I'm damned if I'm going to recommend investment in a company when I've no faith in one of its directors.'

'Then you'd be wrong. Noel is totally trustworthy. He may have overreached himself, but that's only because market forces went against him!' Speedily she went to Noel's defence, stilling the little voice in her conscience that suggested to her that, of the two siblings, Laura had possessed by far the better business acumen. Noel's only fault was he was perhaps a little too trusting—but then that was something she herself could sympathise with!

'My dear Gemma, a successful entrepreneur would have correctly forecast the market forces and taken requisite steps to combat them!'

'And it doesn't take a genius to be wise with hindsight!' she flung back, incensed by his air of superiority.

'Neither does it take one to be aware that love is blind and that you are probably the least able of Noel's associates to form a balanced opinion of his actions!'

'But I'm not in love with Noel...' Horrified, Gemma heard the angrily spoken words leave her lips, and rushed to amplify them before Thor could comment. '...to the exclusion of being able to make an independent appraisal of his business methods.' She stole a sideways look at his profile, praying that her slip had passed unnoticed. A slight dip of his head acknowledged her angry assertion.

'I'll bear that in mind when I come to make a final decision. But don't expect me to throw good money after bad just for old times' sake, Gemma. Whatever you may be thinking, I haven't come here to buy a pardon.'

'I don't know what you mean...' She felt the colour drain from her face.

'Oh, but I think you do, Gemma.' He shot her a quick look before returning his attention to the road. 'But you're no longer seventeen years old. You're a mature woman, experienced in life and love. You've told me you never really loved me, that our affair was simply the springboard to an exciting, fulfilling life, that its dissolution left you with no lasting regrets...'

He paused as Gemma forbore to speak. How could she say anything? Every word he said was true. She had said all those things, intending him to believe them. She still did want him to believe them, didn't she? It was the only way she'd ever be able to free herself completely from his spell.

When he did continue his voice was low, beautifully modulated. 'The fact remains that you do deserve an explanation of events leading to my decision, and, if and when the time is right, you shall have it. I owe you a great deal, my lovely Gemma, but it can't be expressed in financial terms!'

'You owe me nothing!' Her words shook with the passion that tensed her body. 'And as for an explanation... I seem to remember you made yourself perfectly clear five years ago!' She took a deep breath, controlling her mounting fury. 'I should also like to remind you, no one asked you to take an interest in Parangas. It was your own idea.'

'So it was.' The tawny head nodded. 'So you won't hold it against me personally if the decision goes against you?'

Unreasonably, she would. And he knew it. She shrugged her shoulders, 'Does my opinion mean so much to you, Thor?'

'Yes, it does. And I'd like it to be unprejudiced, whatever the outcome.'

'All right.' She considered the matter, too aware of his vital presence beside her to be truly at ease. 'Unprejudiced I shall try to make it.'

'There's a good girl.' He nodded complacently as Gemma sank back in her seat, her sunglasses perched on the bridge of her straight little nose. Behind their anonymity she could try to make sense of what she'd just been through. The only clear thing was that Thor's attitude towards Noel was less than friendly! It would be too absurd to dream that sexual jealousy was at the bottom of it, and Thor had made it quite clear that it was Noel's haphazard business habits to which he objected...but she still had the odd feeling that Thor resented her engagement and would take a malicious pleasure in seeing it founder.

As for an explanation of his betrayal...she was in no mood to listen to a further justification of his wanderlust. It had been a fact of his life and she had accepted it.

An hour of silence between them passed before Gemma directed Thor to turn down a dirt track leading from the road.

'But this is a dead end—there's a farmhouse over there,' he protested, slowing the car down as they approached two five-barred gates secured open.

'Don't worry. It's a right-of-way. The road goes straight through the farmyard. Don't you trust me?' She raised coolly enquiring eyebrows, inwardly amused at his reticence.

'Not entirely,' he told her candidly. 'I have a feeling you'd get a good laugh out of seeing me locked up in a Spanish jail at this moment.'

'You're not far wrong,' she said honestly. 'But I'd have no wish to join you there, and it certainly wouldn't help Noel.'

'Very true.' He considered her set face for a few moments before obeying her instructions, scattering ducks and chickens in his dusty wake as he negotiated the uneven track before emerging on the road again. 'In fact, the most likely thing to help Noel at the present time would be for you and me to call a truce—what do you say?'

'I—I suppose so,' Gemma accorded after a few moments' hesitation. The flare up had been none of her doing, and to prolong it would only do more harm than good. She sighed. It was unrealistic to expect two such different personalities as Noel and Thor to like each other, so if anything positive was to come from their meeting she would have to continue to be the go-between.

'Stop here,' she directed, dragging her thoughts back to the present as she saw the slight break in the undergrowth at the side of the road which indicated the path she had been watching for. 'This is where we walk.'

She didn't mention that it would be a good half-hour's trudge before they even set eyes on the beach and a further ten minutes before they'd negotiated the steep cliff face to reach the sand. He could discover that for himself. And she'd discover if he was as tough as he appeared to be, or whether the tan and the muscles were a disguise for an effete city slicker, after all!

With only beach towels and some cans of lemonade to impede their progress, Gemma led the way, striking out across the scrubland that stretched around them. If Thor hadn't realised the necessity for thick-soled shoes before he certainly would now, she told herself with smug satisfaction, striding out across the sharp, flintlike stones that were packed in among the heavy growth of sweet-scented plants that burst into fragrance beneath their feet.

Already the sun was a power to be reckoned with, burning down from a clear sky, beating its heat against their heads, as they progressed without speaking, only the persistent castanet sound of the unseen cicadas accompanying them every step of the way.

'I hope you like walking?' Gemma enquired sweetly after a quarter of an hour had passed. 'I'm afraid I took it for granted you'd enjoy it.'

'Love it,' he told her easily. Her tone had been sublime, but if he suspected she would have been pleased to see him discomfited by the exercise he didn't betray his suspicion. And there certainly wasn't anything about his long, lazy stride that belied his statement.

'As a matter of fact...' he shot her a quick sideways look and she could see his earlier tension had evaporated

as his mouth curled into an attractive grin '. . . I had to
walk three miles to my first school, so I learned to make
the best use of my legs at an early age.'

Her brow wrinkled as she tried to recall what he'd
once told her about his youth. 'I thought you lived in
Melbourne as a child?'

'Not until I was fourteen.' He measured his stride to
match her own, swinging along easily. 'Before that we
lived in what's referred to as "beyond the black stump".'

'The Outback,' Gemma commented knowingly, sur-
prising herself by remembering this other name for the
Australian bush. Five years ago she'd been so involved
with just being with him, loving him that there had never
been much time for casual conversation. Now she saw
an opportunity of assuaging her natural curiosity and
making the time pass more quickly. 'Were you happy
living in the wilds, Thor?'

'I guess so.' She'd been watching his face and seen the
sudden tautening of his jaw. 'After all, happiness is
comparative, isn't it? At times I used to wish that my
father drank less and my mother smiled more, but like
most kids, on the whole I accepted what I had as being
normal.'

His answer took her completely by surprise. She'd been
thinking in terms of loneliness and deprivation, not of
inter-family squabbles. The bleakness of his terse reply
touched her soft heart.

'I'm sorry, I had no idea,' she murmured awkwardly,
watching the wry twist of his firm mouth as his broad
shoulders lifted dismissively.

'Why should you?' he said mildly enough, but she
could sense some inner turmoil disturbing him as he
kicked away a large stone in his direct path. 'Most people
tend to judge other people's life-styles on the basis of
their own. And from what I saw of yours in England,
it was pretty near perfect.'

For a second Gemma thought he was taunting her about the secure, loving background she'd enjoyed as a child, then she recognised the odd note in his voice as envy rather than sarcasm and relaxed.

'It's something I shall be eternally grateful for,' she admitted quietly. God only knew what would have happened to her if Robin and Stella Carson hadn't come to the rescue of the unwanted toddler, opening both their lovely home and their generous hearts to her. They'd made her so much a part of their close-knit family unit that she'd scarcely given a second thought to her natural mother, who had chosen a new husband in preference to keeping her baby daughter. Only sometimes would she wonder what kind of man would ask such a sacrifice of the woman he loved, and how difficult she had found the choice...

Rather hesitantly, because she wasn't sure whether Thor wanted to pursue this topic of conversation, she enquired tentatively, 'Are your parents still living together?'

'If you can call it that.' The bitterness of his answer was unmistakable. 'They share a house in the suburbs of Melbourne, but their life together isn't anything like as pretty as their surroundings. I guess you'd call it the typical cat-and-dog life—rows and violence interspersed with unnatural periods of calm.'

'Oh, Thor...' There was no mistaking his concern, or the core of anger he experienced acknowledging it. Gemma felt a surge of understanding. Was this why he'd turned his back on her? Had, in fact, never married? Had it been the evidence of his parents' misery that had persuaded him to remain a bachelor?

His tone harshened as he forged ahead over the rocky ground, his eyes narrowed against the glare of the sun, moving with such a distance-eating stride that Gemma was forced to break into a jog to keep up with him. 'My father's a womaniser. The kind of man who makes no secret of the fact he's seeing other women. Oh, he's wealthy and generous enough, but he's no idea of loyalty or discretion. He's systematically tried to break my mother's spirit ever since she first met him.' He turned his head slightly to flick a glance in Gemma's direction. 'You'd like Claudia. Everyone does. She's...' he made a helpless gesture with one hand. 'Oh, it's difficult to describe...'

'Generous-hearted, warm, beautiful...' Gemma suggested softly. 'That's how Dad described her when he used to talk about the old days.'

'Yes.' Thor accepted Gemma's description with satisfaction. 'That just about describes my mother—even now, after all she's gone through.'

'But why doesn't she leave him?' she ventured, encouraged to comment by his frankness.

'You tell me, Gemma.' He halted, swinging round to face her, forcing her by the suddenness of his action to come to a standstill. There was a raw quality in his deep voice that pierced her heart. 'Why is it that some women can overlook the pain their menfolk cause them—not just once, but again and again? What does a woman have that enables her to exercise that divine gift of forgiveness?'

A swift, searching glance traversed her face as Gemma sought to find an answer, suddenly aware that she was being asked to reveal her own emotions as much as guess at his mother's. And the shattering thing was, it would have been so easy to tell him. To confess that women like his mother and like she herself were never able to completely erase love from their hearts. However great the humiliation they were made to suffer, something always remained: a tender root, submerged and unacknowledged, but capable of sprouting into life again and again, given only the slightest encouragement by the man who had brought it into being.

'Well?' he queried, as Gemma felt her mouth go dry with tension, knowing she dared not confide what she'd just discovered, lest Thor realised that she, too, still nourished the remnants of a long lost love.

'A sense of duty, I imagine,' she returned with assumed coolness, and saw from his face that it wasn't the answer he'd wanted.

CHAPTER FIVE

IN THE elegantly styled ground-floor cloakroom of the Hotel Los Angeles, situated on the coast about half-way between Mahón and Ciudadela, Gemma exchanged her bikini for a pair of cool cotton briefs before donning a halter-necked sundress boldly patterned in fondant shades of cream, fawn and orange.

She'd selected the Los Angeles as a lunch stop, knowing the facilities it offered to casual guests were without equal. After a refreshing dip in their salt-water swimming pool both she and Thor had been able to rinse the brine from their hair and bodies under the fresh-water showers provided at the poolside. The heat of the afternoon sun had dried them off in no time, and the luxurious public washrooms offered plenty of space and privacy for a change of clothes.

Meticulously now she began to pay attention to her face, patting in a moisturiser with quick, sure fingers. Common sense rather than vanity had told her that, spending most of her days as she did in the brilliant Mediterranean sunshine, she should ensure the delicate skin of her face didn't dry out and wrinkle like a prune. Usually she didn't bother with other forms of make-up, being blessed with naturally dark brows and lashes, but today, for reasons she didn't care to elaborate to herself, she felt the need to give nature a helping hand.

Mascara lengthened and thickened her eyelashes, a tiny dab of colour at the point of her cheekbones highlighted their curve. Carefully she outlined the pretty bow of her top lip with a dewy peach lipstick, blocking in the light colour before drifting it across the full lip beneath.

The morning on the beach had been superb. As she'd suspected they might, she and Thor had had the entire curve of bay to themselves—a stretch of silver sand flanking a shallow sea of aquamarine clarity.

After Thor's confession of domestic unrest, they'd continued the remainder of the walk in silence until reaching the tortuous path which led down to the beach.

'There you are.' Triumphantly she'd pointed out the pristine, deserted semicircle of sand. 'Was it worth the walk?'

'I'll let you know when I've got my aching feet into the water!' Thor had joked, with no sign of tiredness apparent. 'Come on. What are we waiting for? Give me your hand.'

She hadn't needed a second invitation, reaching out to grasp his warm palm, experiencing a forbidden thrill of pleasure as his strong fingers linked with her own and so many memories fought to claim her attention.

Hand in hand, they'd negotiated the steep track until, reaching the safety of the white sand beach, they'd stripped off their outer clothes to run like carefree children into the warm, refreshing sea.

Gemma drew a comb through her hair, marvelling how quickly it could dry, as she pushed the freshly washed tendrils into place with her fingers. The sea had been like a giant swimming pool, with hardly a tremor disturbing its mirror surface, she recalled blissfully. Content to tumble around in the shallows herself, she watched admiringly as Thor had struck out towards the open sea, moving with a powerful crawl, arms cleaving the placid water, legs moving in a professional, economical paddle.

By the time he emerged, she'd already left the water to spread herself out on her beach towel, the sunglasses perched on her nose serving the double purpose of pro-

tection and disguise. She'd had eyes for nothing else as
Thor had come towards her, water streaming down his
bronzed body, hair burnished gold, she recollected,
feeling a twinge of guilt at the total ambiguity of her
feelings.

In that moment she'd looked at him and loved the
sheer beauty of him. The brief bathing trunks he'd worn
had done nothing to detract from the magnetic power
of his loose-limbed frame, and she'd felt the pulse in
her wrist flutter as her body acknowledged that once
he'd been her lover—her master. The perfection of bone
and muscle and sinew were an accident of nature, her
logical mind told her, meaningless in terms of real merit;
but their balance, their elegance, the sheer mechanical
efficiency of them touched a chord of admiration and
desire deep within her, as she'd fought a losing battle
with her common sense.

Tongue-tied, she'd watched silently as Thor had eased
himself down on the sand beside her, searching in his
beach bag for a can of drink, pulling the ring free and
offering it to her with a grimace.

'It's warm, I'm afraid, but at least it's wet!'

She'd smiled her thanks, gazing up into his face as
she accepted the can. How clear his blue eyes, that could
sparkle with anger one moment only to fill with mischief
the next, how sweet the mouth, with its promise of
sensual pleasure allied to the strong outline of command.
How attractive the rounded chin, with its classical beauty
of Michelangelo's David and its propensity to jut out in
times of stress.

It had taken a great effort of will-power to drag herself
away from the mesmeric effect he was having over her,
but she'd succeeded, reminding herself forcefully that
she was only here to forward Noel's plans, that what
had happened between herself and the splendidly relaxed man at her side was in the past—and that was

where it had to stay if she were to keep her hard-won sanity!

There had been a painful poignancy in Thor's condemnation of his father's philandering. Was it really possible that his personal awareness of what was bred in the bone came out in the flesh that had been the trigger of his sudden flight from matrimony? If so, her parents had been right. It *was* preferable that he left her before the commitment of marriage. Before her adoption she had been an unwanted daughter, jettisoned in favour of her mother's new lover. To be an unwanted fiancée had been devastating, but not as painful as being made to realise that she was a deceived wife!

So they'd lain in the hot sun, sipping their warm drinks and discussing anything and everything that wasn't personal until Thor had asked her, 'Does this beach have a name?'

'Not that I know of.' She'd shaken her head. 'It's said that Menorca has over a hundred and twenty beaches, so it's probable that a few of them don't have a name.' She'd paused before deciding to confide in him. 'As a matter of fact, I call this one the magic beach.'

'Really?' He'd raised himself on one elbow to look down at her. 'Any special reason, or just because it's like something out of a fairy-tale?'

'Yes, it is, isn't it?' She'd felt unreasonably pleased that he saw the place through the same rose-coloured glasses she wore. 'But no, that's not the reason. I call it "magic" because it's not always here. Last year, for instance, it didn't exist.'

Thor's expressively raised eyebrows had invited her explanation.

'It's the winter storms,' she'd explained. 'They can be very violent. The *tramontana* sweeps down from Russia and makes the Med. boil. Sometimes it creates currents that suck all the sand away. Last year that was what happened. All that were left were a few ledges of rock, and the sea itself was much nearer the base of the cliffs. Then, last winter, the situation reversed. The sea brought the sand back, re-created it as it was when I first discovered it five years ago.'

'A powerful magic indeed.' His eyes had been hooded, his voice contemplative. 'It's not very often in life fate deprives you of something, then gives you a second chance to rediscover and enjoy it again.'

The faint mocking inflection in his voice warned Gemma that he was no longer discussing the beach. Alarmed at the deeper implication in his soft tones, she hadn't trusted herself to answer. Instead she'd pretended to catch sight of the time on the waterproof watch that encircled his lean wrist, springing to her feet with false enthusiasm.

'Good heavens—I didn't realise it was so late. We ought to be moving!'

Immediately he'd risen to join her, his movement so swift that she'd started away from him, overbalancing slightly and finding herself caught in his arms as he reached to steady her. It was the very thing she'd sought to avoid! Then, as she'd felt his hands burning into her flesh and smelt the exotic scent of his oiled skin, she'd experienced an overwhelming urge to run her lips across the expanse of sun-baked shoulder so close to them, to savour his taste as she had done once before when his presence had filled her whole universe... Against what was an almost tangible agony Gemma had closed her eyes, an iron self-control holding her body inflexible between Thor's heated palms.

For a few seconds he'd held her unbearably close. Aware of the heavy thunder of his heart, she'd found no strength to break the unwanted embrace. Thigh to thigh they'd stood, the slender satin strip of her scarlet bikini top, long since dry, pressed across the hard, golden

skin of Thor's chest. Then, with a little sigh, Gemma
let her head fall forward to touch his collarbone, feeling
him reciprocate by bending his head to rest it against
her sea-damp hair.

Nothing had been said, and the embrace had seemed
to end by mutual consent. Walking back to the car afterwards, they'd shared a companionable silence. Oddly,
even that had been disturbing, she admitted, giving more
time for the tortuous process of her thoughts. Thor's
presence was as dangerous to her in silence as it was in
speech, she realised with dismay; the pull of the past had
a terrifying power, strong enough to ensnare her even
without his deliberate attempts to exhume their past
relationship.

Gemma sighed, administering a mental slap to her
wayward reflections as she stood away from the mirror,
checking the easy hang of her flared skirt. Satisfied with
her appearance, she reached inside her handbag for the
finishing touch, finding and applying a subtle spray of
Balmain's Ivoire to the pulse points at her throat and
wrist, before replacing her cosmetics in her bag together
with the discarded swimsuit. The fact was, she couldn't
even be sure what Thor's intentions were!

One thing was certain. Today would be the last tour
she'd take him on, the last time she'd expose herself to
his blatant brand of sex-appeal. If his offer to Noel was
genuine, then he'd have to make his decision on what
he'd already seen.

Thor was waiting for her as she emerged into the lobby,
propped casually against a corner of the large reception
desk, light blue jean-style trousers covering his long legs,
a white T-shirt, with broad, pale blue stripes down the
shoulders and sleeves, a snowy contrast to his deeply
tanned face and arms.

'Have you been waiting long?' Schooled from an early
age in the virtue of punctuality, Gemma was cross with

herself for wasting so much time in contemplation. If only she was more able to differentiate between her personal feelings and the cool, businesslike approach she wanted to portray, she might find this day less of an ordeal!

'No.' The startling blue eyes drank in her appearance, lingering on her glowing face, encompassing the soft curves of her breasts beneath their cool cotton covering. 'You look beautiful, Gemma. You're at least twice as lovely as I remembered.'

'Why, thank you, Thor!' The first phase of shock past, Gemma dimpled up at him, fighting against the tide of feeling that surged upwards within her. 'As a matter of fact, this dress of mine is Noel's favourite, and he bought me the perfume for my last birthday.' She didn't wait for his reaction, continuing blithely, 'Shall we go outside and eat? The buffet luncheon is served in the garden restaurant.'

'Lead the way.' Thor released her arm. If he'd sensed how disquieting she found his studied compliment, he'd shown no indication of it. And his tacit acceptance of what she'd claimed surely justified the half-lies she'd told? Noel had never commented on any of her clothes, and although he'd paid for it, she'd been the one to purchase her favourite brand of perfume when he'd declared himself totally without ideas for a gift.

Lunch was a leisurely meal, eaten beneath the shade of strategically planted trees and followed by coffee. Gemma had come prepared to play host, but Thor waved aside her attempt to pay the bill and she quickly decided that discretion was definitely the better part of valour. Any overt opposition on her part could spoil Noel's already slender chances of a successful negotiation, she felt certain.

By the time they'd driven the remainder of the way towards the ecclesiastical capital of the island it was well into the afternoon. Having shown Thor where to park his car, Gemma launched into a spirited history of the Moorish occupation, pointing out the sharp contrast in architecture between the English styled Mahón with its narrow streets, and the gracious palaces and squares of the Moorish capital.

'Mahón has the harbour—Ciudadela has the soul,' she paraphrased, leading him across the main square, which was thronged with excited crowds, to look down on the narrow, twisting harbour where a jousting tournament had just begun as the preliminary to the fiesta celebrations.

'There's not much comparison between the harbours!' he acknowledged with a grin as his gaze travelled along the narrow stretch of shallow water. 'Now I see what they mean when they say berthing a boat in Ciudadela harbour during a storm is like being flushed down a lavatory!'

'So you bought yourself a guide book?' Gemma queried lightly.

'I glanced at one.' Broad shoulders shrugged nonchalantly. 'But I shall get much more out of a personally guided tour.'

'I'm delighted you think so,' Gemma commented drily, refusing to be drawn by his winning smile, and delighted to see the appearance of the mayor on the balcony of the town hall, which saved her from elaborating the point. 'Come on, we're just in time to see the parade of the horses!'

She came to the fiesta every year, and each time she experienced a thrill of magic as the cavalcade of horsemen paraded past the town hall. Coats brushed to a shiny perfection, manes and tails plaited with rainbow ribbons, the high-stepping steeds behaved perfectly under the skilled control of their riders. Each horseman wore a tail-coat, waistcoat, knee-breeches and the traditional two-cornered hat which would be ceremoniously doffed to the mayor as he passed beneath the dignitaries' balcony.

'Here...' Earlier she'd persuaded Thor to buy her a bag of hazelnuts. Now she pressed a handful into one of his palms. 'You have to throw the nuts at the horses' hooves to make them buck and try to unseat their riders.'

'Sounds pretty lethal to me.' Thor started to object then shook his head in disbelief as the scene around them erupted into excited clamour and handfuls of the small nuts sailed through the warm air to assail both horses and riders.

'It does seem pretty hairy,' Gemma agreed, laughing at his expression, 'but casualties are reputedly very rare. The horsemen themselves are incredibly skilled, and the horses are trained to cope with crowds and the missiles. They'll be riding through the crowds for the rest of the day, so you'd better watch out for yourself.'

'It would take more than a horse to scare me...' Thor began easily, only to stop in mid-sentence as a mounted rider came straight towards them. 'Hell, Gemma, look out!' He pushed her forcefully away from his side as the rider pulled his mount inches in front of him, reining the stallion to his hind feet as its forelegs waved in Thor's face before grinning broadly and turning his mount delicately away to pursue another target.

'You were saying?' she queried brightly as Thor passed the back of his hand across his forehead in mock relief, and she returned to his side.

'I was saying I could sure use a beer!'

'That's no problem.' She took his arm. 'The bars and restaurants will be open all day and long into the night. The fun's only just started.'

Taking him to a restaurant-bar in the main square filled with happy Menorcan families, Gemma experienced a quiet sense of satisfaction. By the end of the day she would have taught Thor McCabe a sorely needed lesson.

It was dark and they'd finished an excellent dinner served among the hustle and bustle of excited, friendly crowds when Gemma suggested they finished the day by walking through the narrow streets bordering the main square, knowing what would inevitably occur.

'I see most of the downstairs doors and windows are boarded,' he observed in surprise. 'Are they expecting trouble?'

'Just a precaution,' she returned calmly. 'Down here, I think...'

Almost immediately the dark shadow of a mounted rider detached itself from the surrounding blackness and came full tilt for them.

'This way!' Gemma grabbed Thor's hand and ran, pulling him with her further and further into the dark maze of streets, away from the pursuing horseman, until, turning a corner, they found sanctuary in an unboarded shop doorway. Heart racing, blood pumping furiously through her veins, she listened to the clatter of hooves come to a halt before commencing again to fade into the distance.

'What do you think?' she challenged Thor, eyes sparkling, lips parted with the thrill of the chase. Only this time *they* were the quarry, and it wouldn't end in death and despair.

'A new experience for me,' he admitted, a wry smile twisting his lips. 'I've never been the wrong end of a round-up before.'

'Perhaps you should have been...' Gemma pulled him out into the narrow road, listening for the telltale sounds of hooves. 'Perhaps it will do you good to know what it feels like to be hounded, pressed into a corner, even if it is only make-believe!' A slow-burning anger seemed to ignite within her, as an untypical desire to strike out

at him, to inflict a tiny lash of scorn on his smooth
persona, pervaded her. 'At least even if you do get cor-
nered, no one's going to herd you into a van and slap
a hot iron on you or slaughter you.'

'Gemma—for God's sake!' he responded harshly. 'It
was a job...'

And one that had wrenched him from her side, she
acknowledged, knowing she was being unreasonable, yet
still wanting to strike out and catch him on the raw if
she could. Let him feel what it was like to be a poor
hunted animal.

She twisted away from him as he reached for her,
moving swiftly to the corner of the road, delighted to
see a solitary horseman approaching. Stepping out, she
hailed it—'Hola! Hola!'—then as the rider gathered the
animal's reins, slapped its flanks and sent it at a full
gallop towards her, she started to run, aware that Thor
had joined her.

'OK!' He passed her, seizing her hand and pulling her
along with him. 'If this is what turns you on!' There
was a grim satisfaction on his good-looking face as he
dodged down a narrow alley, eluding pursuit. 'Let me
know when you've had enough of it!'

She wasn't sure if it was the response she'd wanted or
expected, but she had no option now but to continue
the sport. For nearly an hour Thor entered into the spirit
of the fiesta, taking the initiative, leading her deeper and
deeper into the labyrinth of streets, sometimes meeting
and tossing a greeting to other groups of people, sometimes finding themselves alone.

After one chase which had lasted longer than most
and in which they'd only 'escaped' because the horseman
had left them to chase another couple, Gemma found
herself propped up against a wall, shaking with
exhaustion.

'Had enough?' Thor's eyes sparkled in the dim light as he growled his question, his chest heaving with effort.

She nodded. 'Just about.' She turned her head in bewilderment. 'I'm not sure of the way back. Still, if we follow the noise...' She broke off as a solitary horseman appeared, blocking their exit, and she froze against Thor, hoping their immobility would protect them. But even as she watched with bated breath another rider appeared, then another. Three abreast, taking up the full width of the narrow road, so close that the horses' flanks brushed each other with each pace, they began their slow approach.

'Oh, no!' It was a soft moan as Gemma clutched Thor's protective arm. 'I can't run any more!'

'It was your idea,' he chided softly, forcing her to move, pulling her back the way they'd come. 'Come on, Gemma—it's only a bit of fun!'

A few steps towards the only other exit from the street and suddenly there was another horseman barring their way. Gemma stiffened in fright as her heart pounded erratically. As Thor had said, it was fun, a fiesta, nothing was going to happen. Her mind knew it, but the message hadn't reached her body!

'Thor!' Her fingers tightened round his arm as her voice broke on a little sob.

'Quickly...' In response to her unspoken plea he was dragging her along the street, turning abruptly to climb a short flight of steps which his quick eyes must have noticed, and which lead to the entrance hall of a private residence, she presumed as she huddled against the massive, brass-handled door.

On the step beneath, Thor watched in fascination as the solitary horseman continued to approach. He was a young man, his hat long since gone, the glossy neck of his mount flecked with sweat. At the foot of the steps he paused, turning to face them before drawing the animal's front legs high in the air, so that it balanced like a circus horse, its flowing tail pluming behind it.

'Bravo!' Thor applauded a skilful feat of horsemanship. After that, everything seemed to happen at once as, quite calmly, the rider rode his mount up the steps towards them and Gemma screamed, releasing the unbearable tension that enthralled her.

The Spaniard threw back his head and laughed triumphantly as Thor raised one hand in a gesture both protective and conciliatory, and stroked the sable nose of the magnificent animal before him. Then with consummate skill the young rider gentled his steed, against all its instincts, backwards, down the flight of steps. Bowing low, sweeping his arm across in exaggerated obeisance, he turned to gallop away in the direction from which he'd come, closely followed by his three companions.

The next instant, the door against which Gemma had been crouching groaned beneath her and yielded. With a little cry she fell backwards, sprawling on to the hard floor.

'Oh, my God, Gemma—are you hurt?' Thor was beside her, crouched down on the floor, one hand on her arm, the other lifting her chin to enable him to look into her face.

'No, I'm all right,' she hastened to reassure him, but her voice was shaking, and even in the dim light he could see her pallor.

'Can you get up?' He helped her to her feet, concern in every line of his face, every mellow inflection of his deep voice. She was safe now, had never really been in danger, but she'd felt terror and her body had responded to it, pouring out the chemicals into her system that would enable her to fight or run.

Thor was holding her, gazing anxiously into her pale face. She took a deep breath, feeling the adrenalin racing through her system. 'Don't worry. I'm fine.' She smiled up at him, her eyes darkening in apprehension as she read relief and an even more dangerous reaction on his lean face as, instead of releasing her, he drew her more firmly into his arms.

She tried to evade him, but she was no match for his easy strength as he brought his face close to her own.

'Don't fight me, Gemma. We were lovers once...'

She could sense the contained emotion within him, feel it as his body trembled with tension.

'Do you think I've forgotten? That I could ever forget?' Her breath was strangling in her throat as she tried to control the mad pounding of her heart and the tremors that shook her spine. She felt Thor tense as the bitterness she'd been unable to hide accosted him.

'Then don't pretend an indifference you don't feel! Don't lie to me, Gemma!'

His hold on her was almost cruel, but his mouth found hers with unexpected gentleness, moving softly at first with intimate tenderness, warm and erotically persuasive, encouraging her lips to part under his caress: kissing her with a slow, lazy hunger that brought a warm flush of desire to enfold her.

Gemma felt her resistance drain away as the taut power of his legs pressed against her own, making her perfidious body tremble with longing. What on earth had happened to her will-power? The hazy question hovered on the brink of her consciousness. She'd been so determined never to let this happen again, but Thor had trapped her and she hadn't expected the violence of her own reactions. Now she was lost, subjected to and enjoying a slow, sweet, irresistible seduction of her senses.

'Gemma...' Thor raised his head to take a long, shuddering breath before groaning her name. 'Hold me, sweetheart, touch me. Make it like it used to be...'

'No!' It was too much to ask. For five years she'd
tried to obliterate every memory of him. She dared not
awaken the fires of the past in case this time their flames
consumed her entirely. One day she'd meet a man who
really loved her, one who didn't lie and plunder and then
abscond—a man to whom she could truly give her heart
knowing it was a gift he'd value... but not Thor again!
Dear God—not Thor! Her hand flattened against his
shoulder, her body arching in a desperate attempt to
break his hold.

His hands moved—not to release, but to follow the
line of her body as she strained away from him. It was
too much! In resigned despair, Gemma felt her stomach
tighten as her breasts hardened responsively. Unable to
stop herself, she raised her hands to his head, her fingers
tangling in the thick softness of his hair before lowering
them to feel the rough skin of his jaw and the strong
pulse in his neck as she let them drift downwards,
wrapping her slim arms round his body, closing her eyes
and touching once more as if in a dream the rippling
muscles of his back.

Thor uttered a deep, inarticulate noise in his throat
and she felt the heat of his desire as she drew him even
closer to her, lifting her mouth for his kiss, unable at
last to disguise the passion he'd unleashed within her.

This time there was an aching savagery as their mouths
met in a mutual admission of unfulfilled need.

Just as Gemma felt the known world dissolving in disorder about her, Thor broke the embrace.

'It's still there, isn't it, Gemma—the magic between
us?' he asked hoarsely. 'You still have some feeling for
me...' She was still close enough to him in the dim light
to see him swallow. 'You still want me...'

Shattered by what had just happened between them,
Gemma stared at him, accurately reading the daze of
desire that had moulded his features into a heart-stopping

beauty, blindingly aware that his supposition was true. She did still want him. More than that—she still loved him—but she'd never give him the satisfaction of letting him hear her admit it!

'You seem to forget I'm engaged to be married!' she managed, a bitter tightness rising in her throat.

'No more than you do!' Thor's eyebrows met in a thick, dark line over grim eyes, as she cringed from the acidity of his tone.

Heat stained her cheeks as a fiery resentment smouldered in her dark eyes. He'd used his physical superiority to imprison her, and the power he still had as her first mentor in the art of love to suborn her loyalty to Noel. The fact of that loyalty being one of friendship rather than love was beside the point since he knew no different.

'You're hardly a puritan, Thor,' she chided sarcastically. 'So don't go reading things into my behaviour that don't exist. What's a kiss or two at fiesta time? It's all part of the fun, quite meaningless, I can assure you.' She made a point of shrugging her shoulders, and even managed to conjure up a light laugh from somewhere within her aching, frustrated body.

For an instant she imagined she saw naked fury in the gaze he bestowed on her, then he blinked, veiling the expression before she could be sure.

'Fun, hmm?' He repeated her definition thoughtfully. 'Well, if you fancy any more fun in the coming weeks, just let me know. I'll be more than happy to oblige you. In the meantime, are the festivities over for the night, or have you anything else in store for my pleasure?'

She wasn't sure she cared for the cynical double meaning of his question, but then she probably deserved it, she admitted to herself, still shocked by her own lack of self-control, and glad to be able to return to normality without having paid too high a price in loss of pride. 'The fireworks have probably started,' she told him calmly. 'They're a sight not to be missed.'

She followed him from the house, waiting while he reached behind her to secure the door firmly, then she led him back to the Place del Borne, guided by the reports of rockets and the hiss of Catherine wheels.

For over an hour they stood watching the display as fireworks were lit, not one at a time but by the dozen, so that the night sky was ablaze with pink and purple, lime and gold, silver and cerise. Fountains and sprays, cloudbursts, sunbursts—there was everything. The noise and colour were breathtaking, assaulting the senses, leaving the onlookers gasping.

Finally the set piece was lit—a curtain of swinging, sparkling fire, bright golden and ten feet high, surrounding the gracious square.

'Thank you, Gemma.' As the last sparks died away, Thor spoke politely. 'It's been a most enjoyable, instructive day.'

'I'm glad you enjoyed it.' Her mouth was abnormally dry, and the last thing she was going to do was question any ambiguity in his remark.

'What are your plans for tomorrow?' Still the same placid tone, and there could only be one answer now.

'I have to work tomorrow,' she told him brightly. 'One of our waitresses is ill, and I'm afraid I shall be on duty full-time until further notice.'

'I see.'

Beneath the level stare she was subjected to, Gemma felt herself blush, but she persevered, hoping to distract him from the evidence of her uneasiness.

'You must have a good idea by now of what's available,' she floundered on. 'You really ought to drive up to the top of Monte Toro; it's the highest point on the island and the views are magnificent; and I suggest you read that guide book of yours for other ideas.'

'If that's the way you want it.' His mouth was set in a stern line as he began to follow the dispersing crowds, an impersonal hand placed beneath her elbow to guide her. 'Then that's the way it shall be.'

It wasn't what she wanted at all. What she wanted was for Thor to become the tender, loving, faithful man she had once mistaken him for. But she was no longer the innocent, vulnerable teenager of the past, and her faith in miracles had evaporated the day Thor McCabe had broken her heart.

CHAPTER SIX

GEMMA swung one leg over her motor scooter, and alighted, uttering a heartfelt sigh of relief as she parked it neatly against the side wall of the farmhouse. Four days had passed since the fiesta, and Rosa was still under observation in the hospital awaiting a decision from the surgeon as to whether an operation was necessary or not. In the meantime the bar and restaurant had to function. Thank heavens for Josephina! Without the continued help of Leo's sister it would have been almost impossible to cope. As it was, she was being run off her feet as the holiday season gathered impetus.

She sank down wearily on the veranda steps, grateful for a little peace and quiet at last. Since Thor had brought her back here after the fiesta she'd seen nothing of him. Oddly, although she should have been delighted he was keeping his distance, she wasn't! She supposed he must have taken her advice to continue touring the island on his own, but somehow she'd expected he would have shown up during the evening at either Tramontana or La Langousta. It only went to prove, she thought with painful triumph, how ephemeral his interest in her was.

She shivered, although the night air was pleasantly warm. Locked in Thor's embrace that night, all her self-control had vanished. Excitement had run like a fever through her veins, destroying constraint. Thor's power over her had been absolute, and if it hadn't been for the hostile environment in which they'd found themselves, she couldn't bear to think what might have happened!

Dazed with weariness, she pushed her breeze-blown hair away from her forehead. Perhaps she shouldn't judge herself too harshly. After all, the thrill of the chase had sent her blood surging through her veins and released a dangerous quantity of adrenalin into her bloodstream. Under its influence she'd reacted naturally to the masculine authority and pervasive charm of an attractive male. There'd been no real damage done, if one didn't count the scalding pain of memories dredged from some dark limbo in her mind and thrust into the daylight of the present, and since Thor seemed at last to have accepted her ultimate loyalty to Noel, it seemed she might be spared any such further agonies.

She pulled herself heavily to her feet. In all truth, she'd done as much as she could to further Noel's interests. But Thor's personal animosity towards the younger man was hardly encouraging! Deep in thought, she walked through the main door into the large living-room.

'At last!' Noel rose from an armchair to greet her. 'Where on earth have you been, Gem? Do you know it's gone two?'

She managed a teasing grin. 'Good heavens, Noel— you sound like a jealous husband!'

'I was worried about you.' He didn't return her smile. 'You're generally earlier than this. You know how rough the side roads are, and it would be easy enough for you to come off that bike.'

'And you know Tramontana traditionally stays open until the last customer's gone,' she retorted crisply, touched by his concern but irritated at his implied criticism. 'Tonight there was a group of Swedes who lingered on after everyone else had left.' She sighed deeply, suddenly aware how he seemed to have aged in the past weeks, his young face appearing drawn and careworn. 'You shouldn't have waited up.'

'As a matter of fact, I've been going through the
books.' He indicated a pile of ledgers on the table.
'Ramón Casados phoned. Apparently there's some
problem with the bank in Barcelona—it seems they want
interest payments stepped up or they're threatening to
call in their loan.' He picked up one of the ledgers and
slammed it down again, every gesture betraying frustration. 'We're so near—and yet so far!'

Gemma felt her heart sink, persuaded as much by the
terse set of his mouth as by his words, how grim things
were.

'No news from Paris yet, then?' she hazarded,
knowing the payment for the costume jewellery was long
overdue.

'Nothing!' Noel spat the word out. 'I spoke to them
earlier today and all I got was excuses and promises.'
He ran his slim fingers through his unruly hair. 'It's so
unfair, Gem. They could settle their bills on receipt,
they're so damned wealthy. All they're doing is maxi-
mising their investment capital at the expense of poor
devils like us, disregarding the fact that once they've
driven us out of business they're going to have to buy
inferior goods and pay a darned sight more for them
from another supplier!'

Shock kept Gemma momentarily speechless as she as-
similated Noel's angry outburst. She'd never seen him
so utterly disconsolate before. Normally he had so many
irons in the fire that there was always something bright
looming on the horizon.

With an effort, she swallowed down her dismay. 'Is
it really that bad?' she asked solicitously, going across
to him and putting her hand on his arm.

He laughed briefly, without humour, covering the back
of her hand with his palm. 'Probably not, Gem.' He
managed a smile, although it didn't reach his eyes. 'What
do they say—the darkest hour's before the dawn? I guess

things'll look a lot brighter with the sunrise. Besides,' he glanced down at her worried face, 'there's always McCabe!'

Gemma's heart sank, wishing she could share Noel's optimism. She was sure that, whatever his personal feelings, Thor was unlikely to forgo a good profit opportunity; but what if he went over Noel's head to Ramón Casados? Made his offer dependent on the younger man's shares being bought out? She wouldn't put that past this new, more ruthless Thor, and that would be a heart-breaking ultimatum for Noel to face...

'He phoned me this evening,' Noel continued blithely, seemingly unaware of her ambivalent feelings towards his potential saviour.

'And?' Gemma's breath caught in her throat. From what Noel had already said Thor couldn't have turned down his proposition yet.

'He wanted to know if I'd have any objection to his taking you to Sa Salorta one evening as a thank-you gesture for taking him sight-seeing.'

Gemma stared back at him, astonished, her voice trembling as she asked, 'What did you say?'

He shrugged his shoulders, and this time his smile did reach his eyes. 'Well, I did consider playing the heavy fiancé and either saying no, or insisting I joined you, but I finally decided you ought to be allowed to make up your own mind, so I told him you'd get in touch with him. That way it's up to you, isn't it?'

A hundred clashing thoughts spun through Gemma's mind. For the past four days she'd been lecturing herself about keeping her distance from Thor, about never willingly seeking his company. She'd persuaded herself that was the only course to ensure her self-preservation. Now this! She moved away from Noel, her fingers twisting in indecision.

Sa Salorta was a newly opened night club set in the countryside outside Mahón. Originally an old farmhouse, the building had been modernised to accommodate contemporary kitchens and a large, open-air dance-floor had been built. Natural terraces surrounding this had been adapted to take seating, and the whole effect, so she'd been told since she'd never been there to see for herself, was of a Roman amphitheatre, with both food and entertainment being reputed as first class.

'I would like to go there,' she admitted at last.

'Of course you would,' Noel agreed promptly. 'You might even be able to put up with McCabe's company in the circumstances!'

He was teasing her, and not without provocation, she allowed disconsolately. After all, Noel knew her well enough to have registered her distraction since Thor's advent, and to have realised it wasn't based entirely on dislike.

As if he could read her thoughts, the laughter died from his tone. 'Look, Gem, it was your idea to tell him we were going to get married. You've only to say the word if you want to change your mind.'

'No—no, I don't!' She looked at him anxiously. 'Please let it ride, Noel.' God knew, it was the only shield she still had to hide behind!

'OK, if that's what you really want.' He cast her a long, considering look.

'It is.' Gemma turned her head away from Noel's discerning gaze. 'I was a fool a long time ago and I paid the penalty for it. I've learned my lesson, Noel, and it doesn't include a chapter on second chances.' At the door she stopped, looking at his strained face over her shoulder. 'On the other hand, I could use a night out being waited on by someone else, if I can get someone in to cover for me at Tramontana. I'll sleep on his invitation!'

By the time she reached her bedroom she'd already made her decision. In the first place, Thor had behaved with exemplary good manners in making the offer through Noel rather than directly to her. In the second place, he wasn't going to try and seduce her in the middle of a public nightclub, and in the third place, and most importantly, she could use the opportunity to try and find out more about his current attitude towards Parangas.

In the morning she would ring him and accept.

Anyone would think she was a teenager going on her first date! At least she was capable of recognising her own vulnerability and laughing at it! Gemma mocked her own reflection as she deliberately glamourised herself for the evening ahead. What was needed to survive without loss of face was to present herself to her escort in as different a guise as possible from the foolishly devoted virgin she'd been at seventeen.

On the previous two outings she'd been working, accepting a commission. There had been no need to project an image. Tonight was different. Tonight was purely social as far as Thor was concerned, and he should see how much she'd changed since that traumatic parting in England so long ago. Sophistication and a veneer of hardness were what was called for, she determined, using eyeshadow and liner discreetly to emphasise the beauty of her eyes, before standing back from the mirror to cast a critical gaze over her total appearance.

The emerald green silk sheath dress was ideal for Sa Salorta, she decided with satisfaction: not too casual and not too dressy. She dusted her bare shoulders with a sprinkling of golden sparkle before touching her throat and wrists with Ivoire. Yes, that would have to do. Small gold watch, gold pendant earrings—on the point of leaving the room, she hesitated. There was just one more thing she needed. Opening the dressing-table drawer, she took out a small leather jewellery box and removed a solitaire diamond ring from its depths.

Thor would hardly have expected her to wear an engagement ring while she was working or on the beach— but for the evening it was a necessity, if she were to play the role she'd elected. Sliding it on to her ring finger, she experienced a sense of loss as she thought lovingly of her mother, to whom it had once belonged. It was just a little too large, the heavy stone tending to slip sideways on her slender fingers, but there was no danger of it falling off and being lost. If Thor had been misled by her response to him in Ciudadela and thought she would go running to him every time he called the tune, it might serve to remind him the only piper she wanted in her life was Noel! With a satisfied nod, she picked up the small cream clutch bag that matched her high-heeled strappy sandals and went downstairs.

Thor was waiting for her as she entered the living-room, lounging in one of the easy chairs, long legs clad in silver-grey trousers stretched out in front of him, a glass of gin and tonic in his hand.

'I see Noel's been entertaining you.' She smiled a bright, artificial smile as he rose leisurely to his feet, unable to prevent a quick, admiring glance at the pale grey shirt and knotted silk tie which gave him a formal air of elegance.

'I came prepared for a long wait—or even the possibility you wouldn't be coming.' Beneath his light gaze Gemma's whole body seemed to tingle with an unwelcome awareness.

'No.' Calmly she dismissed what she considered a sexist remark. 'If I agree to something, I keep my word. I leave vacillation to others.'

'*Touché!*' Thor inclined his head briefly, but his eyes, coolly calculating, rested on the slight flush of colour painting her cheeks. 'But it wasn't your personal integrity I was challenging. I made allowances for the possibility you might have to work.'

'Oh!' For a moment she regretted her sharp retort. It was a mistake for her to be too prickly. She wanted Thor to think she'd become thick-skinned, didn't she? Which was why she wouldn't apologise. 'I was lucky.' She made a negligent move with her shoulders. 'Josephina produced a niece in her last year at school who was prepared to take orders and generally help out.'

'Then shall we go?' His brilliant gaze swept over her. 'You look stunning, Gemma.'

'Thank you.' She swallowed hastily and looked away. 'I'll just let Noel know we're leaving while you finish your drink.'

Not waiting for his comment, she walked briskly out into the entrance hall, calling Noel's name, irritated that he'd chosen to let her greet Thor without his being there. She couldn't imagine Thor disappearing and allowing the girl he was going to marry go out with another man without a gesture of farewell. Come to that, she couldn't imagine Thor countenancing his wife-to-be going out with another man anyway! She could still remember how possessive her Australian lover had been during their own relationship, despite its short duration.

'We're leaving now, Noel.' Thor was just behind her as Noel came down the stairs. Purposefully she went forward, towards the younger man, arms outstretched, eyes pleading for his co-operation.

'Enjoy yourself, darling.' Noel picked up his cue perfectly, hugging her warmly and kissing her on the cheek, restraining her with a firm arm round her shoulders as she would have walked away.

'Take care of her, McCabe,' he instructed tautly, an unexpected sternness in his tone lending it an untypical authority, before he released his grip and allowed her to walk towards Thor.

'Oh, I intend to, Shelton. I assure you.' It was a lazy drawl, as if something about the situation amused him. 'Don't forget, Gemma and I go back a long way.'

Three hours later, sipping champagne and listening to a top-flight cabaret artiste singing about the man she'd loved and lost, Gemma mused on the perfection of the surroundings. There could be few more romantic settings, she pondered, than the natural amphitheatre nestling amid the gentle hills beneath the starlit night of a Menorcan summer. As a stage set it was flawless, and that was just how it felt to her—contrived and unreal.

As the *chanteuse* bewailed her lost love, Gemma questioned her own expectations of the evening. Certainly not the polite and impersonal conversation she and Thor had indulged in up to that time, she decided! It was as if the formality of his dress had affected her escort's manner. Thor couldn't have behaved with more propriety had Noel been sitting there with them!

She took a surreptitious glance at the diamond ring on her finger, well aware that Thor had observed it but had chosen not to comment. By wearing it she seemed to have turned the date into a threesome. But wasn't that what she'd intended? Brutally honest with herself, she admitted she'd wanted it to act as an amber light if Thor showed any signs of increasing the intimacy of their acquaintanceship beyond what she was prepared to accept. But it seemed he'd taken it as a red light: denying her the compliments and casual flirtation she'd anticipated in a social evening, treating her instead with a distant courtesy.

She closed her eyes, letting the words of the song drift over her. That she felt disappointed could only be to her shame. She was being desperately illogical, and all because of the conflict between her physical attraction for Thor and the need to maintain her emotional, one could almost say 'spiritual', integrity.

The song ended on a sustained note, and a warm burst of applause greeted its finale.

'Would you like a brandy or liqueur, Gemma?' He was the perfect host. Thor's blue eyes glinted, sparklingly alive in contrast to the lazy, soft sound of his Antipodean drawl as he leant slightly forward across the table.

'No, thank you.' She could match his politeness any day. 'It was a lovely meal, and I think I've had enough champagne to drink as it is.'

'I'm glad you enjoyed it.' His cool, level gaze was somehow unnerving, or it could have been because she was so unnaturally tense. 'It was the least I could do after the two most enlightening days you shared with me.' His eyes mocked her as the atmosphere between them became charged with innuendo.

'I'm delighted you enjoyed what I had time to show you of the island,' Gemma said demurely. 'Am I to understand you were impressed with what it had to offer?'

'Oh, very impressed.' Thor's gaze dwelt consideringly on her flushed cheeks, as she silently dared him to affront her with another *double entendre*. 'I agree there's still potential here to be realised.'

Eagerly Gemma seized on what she saw as a favourable comment. 'Of course, I don't imagine it's anything like as beautiful as your own island on the Reef...'

Catching and holding her anxious gaze, he stared intently into her dilated pupils. 'But then it has one thing my island can't offer—history. I took your advice and drove around and eventually discovered some of the Bronze Age monuments the guide books refer to—

taulas—I think they're called.' A raised eyebrow invited her confirmation.

'Incredible, aren't they? Engineers still don't know how it was possible for such an early civilisation to get a stone thirteen feet long and five feet wide to balance on another one sixteen feet in height when even the most primitive lifting devices were unknown.' Gemma's eyes sparkled with enthusiasm. 'What fascinates me is that they were quite old when Xuroy was living in the caves. They would have been just as common a sight to him as to us!'

'Yeah...' Thor nodded his head sagely. 'It gives a different perspective to time lapse, somehow, don't you think? I mean, compared to the light of day the *taulas* have seen, five years is no more than the blink of an eye, is it?'

Gemma glanced at him uncertainly, her mouth suddenly dry, as she identified a silky note in the question which alarmed her. She felt her pulse quicken and wished she'd had slightly less champagne. However, she wasn't going to allow Thor's smooth reference to their personal past to deter her from her purpose. Since she could think of no subtle way to approach the subject so dear to her heart, she took a deep breath and plunged in.

'Have you made any firm decision about Parangas yet?'

'Is that the only reason Noel agreed to your accepting my invitation—so you could ask me that?'

Beneath his intent regard she could feel her heart pounding, an angry tautness holding her spine rigid. 'I don't have to ask Noel's permission about what I do or where I go...' She paused, the fingers of her right hand twisting and turning the heavy diamond gracing its partner.

'Or with whom?' he queried gently.

'Or with whom!' Gemma confirmed coldly. 'Noel and I share an open and trusting relationship.' Which was true, she comforted herself silently, before continuing boldly, 'The days when women asked their men for permission to live their own lives have long since gone by. Or hasn't that news reached Australia yet?' Her lovely chin lifted defiantly, as she saw a small flame of anger flicker across Thor's hard-boned face. Probably, she decided with a thrill of satisfaction, he wasn't used to being taken to task by a woman. Didn't the Aussie male have a reputation for New World *machismo* of the worst kind?

'Too right it hasn't!' He gave her a breathtaking smile, carelessly removing the sting from her attack by refusing to defend himself. 'Back home we still keep our Sheilas in their rightful places—the kitchen, the bedroom and the laundry-room!'

Despite herself Gemma felt her mouth twitch, the sentiments themselves no more outrageous than the exaggerated 'Strine' in which they'd been voiced, stirring her sense of humour.

'That's better.' Thor approved her retreat from the attack. 'But before I answer your question let me ask you one. How long have you been engaged to Noel?'

For a moment Gemma sat staring at his mildly enquiring expression, as if suspended in a void. Dear heavens—it was something she'd never even thought about. What would seem reasonable. A period neither too long nor too short?

'About a year,' she said at last.

'About?' An ironic lift of an eyebrow mocked her inexactitude.

'A year on the twelfth of next month,' she amended coolly.

'After living with him for four years?'

'At first I simply shared his house with him and his sister Laura.' She was indignant at his curiosity, but unwilling to refuse him an answer if Noel's future depended on her verbal co-operation. 'By the time Laura left to get married, our relationship had grown beyond friendship.' Her sparkling eyes defied Thor to comment adversely.

'Not exactly love at first sight, then?'

Gemma looked at the sardonic expression on his intent face and guessed he was deliberately baiting her for some purpose of his own.

'No, it wasn't,' she agreed curtly. 'I'm a quick learner. I now know the difference between mere physical attraction and the deeper, lasting emotion of true love.' She paused, studying the strong face of the man she had once loved to distraction—the dark brows, the straight nose above the shapely, determined mouth, the aggressive line of the rounded chin. He was watching her with concentrated interest and she knew she had to go on. Despite her resolution, she couldn't completely hide the tremor in her voice. 'Noel is kind and considerate and gentle,' she declared, the ring of truth in her voice. 'He's good-tempered, easy to live with and I can trust him!'

'And you love him very much,' Thor prompted her softly.

'And I love him very much!' she echoed forcefully, since Thor had left her no other option. And it was the truth. She *did* love Noel, not as she'd once loved the man who sat opposite her, but as a friend, a man who had never let her down when she needed his support.

Thor's gaze swept across her mutinous face, seeing the defensive look in her eyes, the challenging tilt of her chin, the proud lift of her soft mouth, and nodded his head thoughtfully.

'Then, for the sake of your future happiness together, I'll pursue the possibilities it offers. But it's not a decision I can make unilaterally. There's far too great a sum of money involved. Fortunately Edmund Curran, my business partner Down Under, is cruising his own yacht round the Med. this summer and I've already managed to contact him. I expect him to be in Mahón within the next few days.'

'But that's marvellous!' She leaned across the table, her lips parted with pleasure, her eyes glowing with relief. 'Will he like it, do you think?'

'Well, it's no coral atoll . . .' He regarded her eagerness with sombre amusement. 'But I imagine he'll be guided by what I have to tell him.' He pushed back his chair, rising lazily to his feet. 'And now, how about joining me on the dance-floor?'

Held lightly in Thor's arms, moving slowly to the romantic music, Gemma closed her eyes, enjoying the possessive touch of his fingers on her back, the strong pressure of his thigh as he guided her to his will. Gradually her body moved closer, familiarising itself once more with the vital masculine frame it remembered so agonisingly clearly as Thor's arms tightened their hold. As her breasts were pressed against his muscular chest, she could feel the heavy thud of his heart. Automatically her hands rose to encircle his neck, his head lowered, and they were unashamedly dancing cheek to cheek in the dim light beneath the velvet-dark sky.

Just the scent of his skin was enough to inflame her, to send a stream of molten fire sweeping through her body, so that the blood in her veins sang with excitement and her nerves tingled with expectation, as her heart pounded with the sound of his name— Thor . . . Thor . . .

This would be the last time she'd hold him close. Who could blame her if she made the most of it? In a few weeks he'd be gone from her life again. Only this time she'd ensured his passing would not devastate her—only leave her a little scorched.

CHAPTER SEVEN

'CAN I offer you a coffee?' Thor switched off the ignition and turned to face her.

It had been the early hours of the morning when they'd left Sa Salorta, and Gemma had supposed he intended to drive her straight back to her home, but the entrance road to El Dorado lay a little off the main road between Mahón and San Luis, and she'd sat beside him wordlessly as instead he'd turned the car towards the Villa Sabina. If she'd wanted to protest she should have done it at that moment. Now it was too late. She had given her tacit approval to the re-routeing and would have to face the consequences.

Not that she would have to face anything she couldn't handle, she encouraged herself silently. The Thor she'd known and loved in the past had never been a violent man. Positive and determined, yes, but never one to use physical force against a woman, and despite her better judgement she still felt an inexplicable longing to enjoy his company for a few more precious minutes.

Something of her inner struggle must have shown in her face, as Thor added gently, 'We need to talk, you and I.'

'All right,' Gemma agreed, keeping her voice steady, unable to prevent herself from colouring as his eyes left her face to rest on her hands, his mouth tightening ominously as he witnessed the stressful way she was manipulating the ring on her finger.

She allowed herself to be led towards the villa and on to the flat roof where they'd lunched that first day.

Shielded wall lights cast a pleasant soft glow over the leisure furniture that had replaced the previous dining-set—a luxurious swinging hammock and two matching sunchairs. A low, oval table was already laid with a tray containing coffee-cups and a bowl of wrapped sugar lumps and dairy creamer, while an electric percolator stood waiting to be plugged in.

It appeared Thor had already prepared for company, Gemma decided, as she observed the two additional brandy glasses and a bottle of cognac which shared the table.

'Come and sit down, Gemma.' It was more of an order than a request as, having switched on the percolator, Thor sank down on the hammock, holding out a welcoming arm towards her.

Ignoring his gesture, she chose to subside on one of the chairs, disturbingly aware of a magnetic pull that seemed to drag her towards him, and determined to fight it.

'What's the matter?' Thor's brilliant gaze pinned her, intimate, pointedly self-confident. 'You've been in my arms for a good part of the evening, but it seems you can't bear to sit next to me now we're alone?'

Yes, she'd been in his arms, felt his tough male skin against her own soft cheek, and the experience had sapped her will-power. Already she was beginning to regret her rash behaviour in allowing him to bring her back to the villa. Yet she must be careful not to provoke a scene which could ruin Noel's plans before they'd even been presented to Ed Curran.

'That was different,' she muttered. 'I'm sorry, Thor, but I don't think I should stay for coffee, after all. Noel will be expecting me back.'

'But then, you're a free agent, aren't you, Gemma?' came the cool retort. 'Mistress of your own destiny—

free to indulge yourself in a little fun when the fancy takes you, hmm?'

Beneath his steady gaze her resolve faltered. He was using her own words against her, and for a moment she could find no easy defence against his insinuations...unless she dared plead the ubiquitous headache!

Instead she decided to fight fire with fire, meeting his quizzical regard with an assumed confidence she was far from feeling. 'Unfortunately for you, tonight the fancy doesn't take me. I can only apologise if I gave you any reason to believe that it did.'

As the percolator began to buzz she switched it off and calmly poured out two cups of coffee, handing one across the table to Thor with a steady hand. 'Still, I guess I can spare another ten minutes to enjoy your hospitality, rather than risk offending you.'

'Offending me!' Beneath level brows he regarded her, mocking her useless attempt to deny the tension building between them, his eyes absorbing every detail of her lovely face. 'Whatever kind of word is that to use between the two of us? I thought we'd agreed to be friends.'

For an electric moment her anger outweighed her reserve, then Gemma forced herself to relax. 'It's been a long time since we were close...' It wasn't the best way of putting it, but 'close' was a better word than 'intimate' in the circumstances, so it would have to do. 'Our lives have diverged enormously since we both left England.' She made a small gesture with both hands. 'People change, and friendship doesn't always survive those changes.'

'And you think I don't know that, Gemma? That the same thought didn't haunt me from the time I decided to come here and find you again? That I didn't spend my first three days on the island wondering if you would be changed beyond all recognition, if the girl I had known in England might have gone for all time?'

'You came because my father told you about Parangas...' she protested, unwilling to face the facts he had thrown at her.

'I came because of you, Gemma!' he snapped, his eyes as hard and brilliant as sapphires. 'I wanted to see you again, to find out if there was anything left of the passion we once shared.'

To what purpose? But it was a silent cry, as Gemma's resolve to remain uninvolved teetered on the brink of submission. Thor still wanted her, and God knew, she wanted him. Would it be so disastrous to spend just this one night recapturing the splendours of their young love? Hadn't she matured enough to be able to cope with the anticlimax of the morning after?

'Gemma?' Just her name, in Thor's soft whisper, but it asked a hundred questions, none of which she was prepared to answer truthfully. Instead she moistened her lips determined to stand by her original decision while she still had the strength to do so.

'And you discovered that life doesn't stand still, that the little girl you once knew had grown up and was about to be married.' She forced herself to smile slightly. 'You surely didn't imagine I was still living in the past, Thor?' she chided gently. 'Any more than I can believe you gave up chasing women completely in the interest of chasing cattle.' She raised an interrogative eyebrow, inviting his amusement.

'I don't chase women!' Anger flickered briefly through his eyes.

Of course he didn't. Gemma silently accepted his denial. When a man had a physical presence, like Thor McCabe, he wouldn't need to stalk his prey. There were plenty of other women, like herself, who would be enchanted by his gloriously fit body and attractive face;

who would dream of being held in those strong arms and kissed by that firm silky mouth; and who, unlike her, would settle for the physical ecstasy of his love-making with no emotional rapport.

'My mistake,' she murmured softly, reaching for her coffee.

'Dammit, Gemma!' His mouth tightened inexorably. 'I told you there's never been another woman in my life that I've taken seriously!'

'So you did,' she agreed equably, her eyes darkly intent, surveying him over the rim of her cup.

'While you, of course, have played the field!' His voice roughened, stripping her hard-won courage, a terrible coldness holding her in its thrall as the abrasive words tore at her heart; but she'd already implied as much to him at an earlier meeting. In a strange way, refusing to deny the implication made her feel less vulnerable.

'Be realistic, Thor. This is a holiday island. The opportunities for romance are legion, and a great many very attractive ships pass this way in the night.'

'But none as attractive as Noel, it seems,' he grated.

'That's right.'

With commendable calm, Gemma took another sip at her coffee as Thor pushed himself up from the hammock with impatient force, thrusting his hands into his pockets and striding towards the parapet surrounding the sun roof, to stare out over the dark waters of the lake.

'You tell me you've been engaged for nearly a year,' he shot back accusingly over his shoulder. 'Your father never mentioned it to me when we talked about you.'

'Perhaps he didn't consider it any of your business!' Sharply, Gemma admonished his impertinence, before relenting. 'On the other hand, it was probably because he doesn't know.'

'You mean he wouldn't approve? He doesn't like
Noel?' Thor came towards her, standing over her so she
was forced to tilt her chin to address him.

'Not at all!' she told him sharply. 'In fact, Dad's never
met Noel, although he knew his sister Laura quite well
because the two of us were at school together. When
Laura left the farmhouse to get married, Dad knew Noel
and I intended to continue sharing, and he accepted that
it's quite common nowadays for couples of mixed sexes
to share accommodation without being otherwise involved with each other. But if I were to tell him that I
was going to marry Noel, he'd assume correctly that we
were already living as man and wife—and I think that
would distress him. So we agreed to spring our news on
him this autumn when we shut down the restaurants and
return to England to arrange the wedding.' The glib explanation slid smoothly from her tongue.

Thor stared down at her, his expression enigmatic.
'Your father didn't strike me as being narrow-minded.'

'He's not!' she rushed to Robin Carson's defence, unwilling and unable to explain the depth of her love and
admiration for the man who had given her his name and
his home and his enduring affection. 'It's just that he
tends to be more than usually protective of me, and I'd
hate to be a disappointment to him, or give him unnecessary worry.'

It was why she'd never confided in either of her parents
that she'd allowed herself to be seduced by their plaus-
ible Australian visitor. Her own pain had been hard
enough to bear; to carry the weight of Robin and Stella's
hurt on her behalf would have been a monstrous burden.
As it was, she'd fled to Menorca rather than let them
observe just how badly she was bleeding from the cut
of Thor's renegement...

She dragged her mind away from the tragedy of the
past to discern Thor's eyes narrowed on her with a

passionate intensity which caused an unbidden tremor to tremble through her limbs. 'All your father wants is your happiness, Gemma...and so do I...'

Before she realised his intention, he'd reached down, seizing her arms and drawing her to her feet. 'I may be wrong, but I don't believe it lies with Noel.'

'You *are* wrong!' she cried out furiously, aware that she was trembling, as panic flooded through her. 'What do I have to do to convince you?'

'Nothing.' His fingers tightened on her arms. 'Just let me convince myself.'

She couldn't have stopped him if she'd wanted to at that moment, and, to be honest, she wasn't sure she did. Thor's head lowered, his mouth, hard and warm, targeting on her soft lips, persuading them to open with a determined seduction of her senses that left her gasping.

'Gemma, my sweet love,' he muttered thickly, his breath warm on her cheek, 'you can't have forgotten how good it used to be between us...'

She sensed the ruthless hunger consuming him, and discovered it arousing an answering heat in her own body that left her weak and yielding. She'd never intended this to happen, yet in its own way it had been inevitable, and every moment she was becoming less able to fight the dominance Thor was exerting over her.

His breath rasped against her neck as his burning lips trailed a path down her throat with a possessive, demanding passion that made her pulse leap with a wild excitement. No, she had forgotten nothing. The years between ceased to exist as her body flowed against his hard frame, her breasts flattened against his powerful chest, the sweet cradle of her hips spreading to contain the virile thrust of his unashamed masculinity.

But it had never been quite like this... Gemma's hands twisted in his tawny, gold-streaked mane as Thor's voracious mouth caressed the tender swell of her breasts above her silken neckline and his hands moved convulsively on her hips, pressing her so close to himself that she fancied she could hear the thunder of his heart as his breath sawed in his chest. Five years ago he had been gentler; now there was a turbulence in his actions, as if meeting her again had unleashed a primitive power hitherto unrevealed. It terrified and exhilarated her, conjuring up a fiery elation she'd never experienced before.

'Do you remember, my love? Tell me you remember...' His palms moved in urgent supplication over the supple curves of her pliant body as his voice, deep and husky with unrestrained passion, demanded her confession.

Intoxicated by his kisses, her body melting in his arms, Gemma couldn't lie.

'I remember, Thor...I remember...'

It had been good, oh, so good! That first time she'd been nervous, loving him desperately, wanting nothing more than to be the instrument of his satisfaction. She'd been totally without experience, eager and responsive, but naïvely afraid he would find her attempts to give him pleasure disappointing. She'd never even considered the trauma her own body might receive, had been prepared for discomfort...even pain, her anxious mind trying to recall the books she'd read, searching her memory for applied knowledge to compensate for her lack of real experience.

In the event it was Thor who had led her, step by incredible step, into a world of sensual pleasure the existence of which she'd never dreamed. With gentleness and passion and time, he'd introduced her to the secrets of her own body, bringing her to a mind-shattering, shuddering climax. At the time she hadn't even realised the nature of the source of pleasure he'd unlocked within her. She'd only known that afterwards, when for the first time he'd claimed her totally with his own body, possessing her smoothly and effortlessly without pain, and she'd been so grateful she'd concentrated her whole being on reciprocating his gift.

When he'd cried aloud before collapsing, shuddering, against her, for one frightful moment she'd supposed she'd hurt him in some way. Then, when he'd opened his eyes and seen her tears and avowed the depth of his own ecstasy, she'd shed even more tears...

Then, a month later, when she was aglow with the excitement of becoming his legal wife, contemplating with a fierce joy the prospect of bearing his children, he'd told her he had never really loved her...

'It can be like that again, Gemma.' Like Satan he tempted her now, crooning enticingly into her ear. 'I want you so badly...' His voice deepened, became a groan. 'I could never get you out of my mind, out of my blood.' He was trembling, his strong body quivering with unbearable tension. 'I thought I'd lost you for ever, then I went to England for the funeral and met your father again and he told me all about you, how you were living in Menorca with a friend... and I had to come, to find out for myself if you still felt anything, anything at all for me.' His voice broke. 'Dear God, Gemma—ever since you walked out of Tramontana like a ghost from the past I've ached for you...'

Tormented with a raw need to recapture that past ecstasy, if even for a fleeting moment, Gemma felt her resolve waver. She couldn't doubt Thor's sincerity. His whole lean, supple frame was primed with the powerful energy of predatory man, but was he offering her anything other than a repetition of heartbreak?

It had taken weeks to school her body into accepting his loss, months to stop his image invading her dreams, years to rout out every scrap of love for him from her heart... No! She was fooling herself. She had never ceased loving him.

'What do you want from me?' she whispered in an agony of indecision.

'Everything, my darling.' Ardent as ever, he made no compromise. 'Everything you've got to give me! Gemma, listen to me.' His eyes smouldered as they lingered on her upturned face. 'Seeing you again like this, being with you, yet having to watch another man kiss you, is tearing me apart. I want your love and your trust, Gemma—but I've forfeited the right to ask you for either... and if all you've got left to offer me is the consolation of your sweet body, then stop punishing me for the past, my darling. Stop punishing both of us, because your skin beneath my fingers tells me quite a different story from your cold little voice in my ear!'

Reluctantly his arms surrendered their hold, freeing her from his embrace. 'It's your decision, Gemma. I won't even try to persuade you again. If you walk away from me now, I'll drive you straight back to Noel. But if you stay...' He left the sentence unfinished as he watched the shadows chase across her mobile face.

Gemma hesitated for only a moment, before she accepted that there was only one way she could act to keep faith with herself. Conscious of the strain which tensed his jaw, she heard his sharp indrawn breath as she turned on her heel, pushing aside the heavy glass doors to enter the house.

'I'll get the car...' he said tersely, only yards behind her as she reached the centre of the room.

'Why?' She prayed her nervousness didn't show in her voice. 'Are you going somewhere?'

Somehow she reached the far side of the room, pausing beside the dressing-table to slide the diamond ring from her finger, depositing it in a small glass tray before raising both hands to detach her earrings and send them clinking down beside it.

'Gemma?' Thor's voice sounded as dry as her own parched throat, a note of wonderment in it, as if he couldn't believe what he saw. But he would...

She smiled at him, a breathtaking sparkle of allurement as she reached her fingers to the long zip at the back of her dress, slowly drawing it down until she could step from its fallen folds. Beneath it she'd worn an oyster satin bodyshaper, low-necked, high-cut in the leg. Carefully now, with fingers that shook, she lowered its thin straps, the liquid softness of her pupils fixed on Thor's face as she drew the delicate garment down her body. She would stay—but on her own terms—because she wanted to. He could have her body, and she'd make sure he remembered it for the rest of his life! He would have her love, too—but she'd make sure he never guessed the magnitude of her emotions.

She saw him swallow, saw the glazed look that transformed his face, was aware of the hardened contours of his vital male body and felt an answering need within her own body well up to meet the desire he had no chance of hiding from her.

In the privacy of the farmhouse, she'd spent her snatched leisure time sunbathing with only a minimum token garment to preserve her modesty, with always a wrap to hand for an unexpected emergency. As the oyster satin whispered to the floor she stood before Thor, her first, her only lover, her youthful body the colour of honey, save where the tumid apices of her breasts turned mulberry pink.

'I've decided to stay a little longer,' she told him simply, her coolness evaporating as with a muffled groan he swept her into his arms, burying his face between her breasts, whispering an unintelligible jumble of half-phrases as he kissed every satin inch of skin within reach of his hungry lips.

Kneeling on the bed above her, Thor lowered her gently on to the pillows of the double bed. It seemed he was making a valiant attempt to control the urgency that blazed from his eyes, exercising a beautiful control in the way he caressed her, so that sensuous shivers trembled up her spine.

Reaching towards him, Gemma pulled his shirt away from his trousers, stroking the fine skin of his back, teasing the golden hair across his shoulders, fingering the hard nipples on his chest, watching his shuttered face, seeing the effect it had on him; knowing that even while her own body responded to his touch she was beginning to lift him on to the path of fulfilment.

She smiled lethargically at his entranced face, the dark sweep of his lashes making him look like a tired child. Brushing the thick, tawny hair from his forehead, she retraced the outline of his features with her fingers, following their path with soft, butterfly kisses, frightened and excited by the contrast between the lazy innocence of his face and the threat latent in his strong male body with its power, its stamina and its inherent drive to procreate.

Clinging to him, she accepted his deepening kiss, conscious of the rougher texture of his jaw against the palpable softness of her own satin skin. This might be a game, an interlude for Thor. For her it was to be one final journey into the Paradise she'd lost . . .

'Why, Gemma . . . why?'

For a moment she thought she was imagining the tortured question, but he repeated it, his voice hoarse and broken.

'Why do you want me?'

It was like being dunked under a cold shower as she felt the tide of warmth ebb away from her body.

'You want a reason?' Horrified that he could have broken the spell they'd been weaving, she could only stare at his anguished expression, hear the breath rasping in his throat.

'Yes. I want a reason.' His face only inches above hers, he stared down unblinking into her dilated pupils. 'Am I just another summer affair—or is this something special?'

Oh, how dared he? Choosing her weakest moment to try and wring out a confession of love from her, an admission that there had been no other man in her life—not even Noel. What a triumph that would be for the man who had toyed so cruelly with her youthful affections! What a boost for his male ego when he returned to his island in the Coral Sea. No! It wouldn't happen that way. She would retain the independence she'd fought so hard to win.

'Of course it's special.' She fluttered her eyelashes in a travesty of seduction, as her quick brain presented the perfect answer to preserve her susceptibility. 'It's the price of getting your approval on Parangas, isn't it?'

She saw his face change and felt a thrill of satisfaction at stimulating his anger, followed immediately by a sensation of real fear. She'd only seen Thor really enraged once before in her life. That had been when a teenage cyclist had run into her on a crowded pavement. He'd collared the unrepentant boy and told him exactly what he thought of him, although she'd only been shaken rather than hurt. As an onlooker she'd been embarrassed and shocked both by his language and his attitude; later she'd accepted his justification in administering a tongue-lashing. After all, the cyclist's next victim might have been an older person or a young child, and the damage to them much greater.

Now, recalling his scathing anger, she began to regret the rashness that had prompted her into such a retort.

By putting their proposed lovemaking on a commercial basis, she had surely renounced any claim to either gentleness or understanding in what was about to follow.

Staring at him bleakly, Gemma saw contempt replace the dreamy look of desire in his eyes, and winced as his mouth set in a line so stern that it was impossible to believe that only seconds previously she'd teased its sensuous curves with her own soft lips.

'You think I was making sex with you a prerequisite of getting your boyfriend out of trouble?' He moved away from her, regaining his feet to stand staring down at her as if she was some unsavoury specimen he'd found on the beach.

Instinctively she backed away from the heat of anger that had turned his eyes to chips of blue ice, and saw him suck in the corners of his mouth impatiently as he caught her movement.

'You were actually prepared to indulge me because you thought I'd finance your lover's plans as a token of my gratitude?' He was tucking his shirt back into his trousers, from whence her eager fingers had recently plucked it.

Confused by the strength of his reaction and irritated by his clinical description of what had been about to happen between them, Gemma refused to recant.

'And what if I was?' she asked huskily. 'You wanted to...' she hesitated, then boldly used his own description, 'to have sex with me. You can't deny it.'

'Nor would I choose to if I could.' The statement held no softness. 'You honestly believed I'd turn Noel's plan down flat unless you co-operated? That *that* was the reason I brought you back here?'

'Wasn't it?' her tone challenged him. It wasn't what she'd thought, but it was feasible, and she wasn't about to back-track now. Surely Thor would have delighted in such a bargain—an arrangement that wouldn't put him under any personal obligation to her? He'd shied from commitment once before, hadn't he? She met his cold appraisal squarely, her heart sinking as she began to believe in her own wild accusation.

'Well, he certainly merits your lack of faith in his project, if not your devotion to his cause,' he allowed cruelly.

It was as if a core of ice had taken over her heart as he made no attempt to deny her allegation. She'd asked for it, and now she found his tacit agreement more belittling than either rage or passion, as his lazy, arrogant eyes travelled slowly over her revealed body. He made no attempt to hide their admiration, but there was no kindness in their blue depths.

'You're a very beautiful woman,' he told her with careful deliberation. 'But there's one thing you should know. If I want a physical encounter with a female of the species I don't have to pay for the privilege. I don't have to pour a small fortune into a teetering business just for the transitory pleasure of a night's fun!' The harsh voice continued inexorably. 'Be grateful I asked you for a reason, Gemma, or you could have awakened a very disappointed woman in the morning!'

Only the memory of the suffering she'd once endured at his hands lent her some dignity as Gemma reached for the clothes she'd discarded on the floor. Her body was aching and unfulfilled, her dreams shattered, but she wouldn't let Thor see how deeply she had wounded herself. He watched her carefully, his face devoid of all expression. 'Tell me, did Noel know the extent of the sacrifice you were prepared to make on his behalf? Did he in fact suggest it, hmm?'

'No!' She was truly horrified that her incautious comments had irrevocably maligned the man who had befriended her when she'd most needed it. 'I don't discuss everything with Noel; we're not...' She stopped, aghast.

In her rush to absolve him she'd nearly said 'we're not lovers'. Now she amended the sentence. 'We're not in each other's pockets.' She clutched her clothes to her body as she spoke, shielding her nakedness from the withering scorn she saw etched on Thor's personable face.

'I must say I'm impressed by the lengths to which you were prepared to go to help him, then. Perhaps I've misjudged Noel Shelton, after all. It seems he must have hidden depths to have earned such fidelity.'

Bitterly she glared at his censorious face. 'What would someone like you know about fidelity, Thor?'

She saw his eyes close briefly and his face tense as if she'd hit him, then he said tersely, 'What, indeed?' before he turned his back on her, moving towards the door and pausing on the threshold. 'Get your clothes on, Gemma. I have to go out for a short while. When I return, I'll drive you back to your fiancé.' He left her without a second glance.

Alone she obeyed him, pulling on the flimsy undergarment over her heated flesh, smoothing down the crumpled silk of her dress. She truly hadn't expected so sharp a reaction. What she'd witnessed had been a tightly controlled anger, condensed by will-power to a concentrated spear of anger with the searing quality of a laser beam! No wonder she felt as if she'd been scalded all over.

Thor had felt used! It was such a bitter irony that she couldn't stop the burning tears welling in her eyes from coursing down her cheeks. She hadn't cried like this for five years! All that time she'd imagined she'd exhausted her own personal well of unhappiness. Even when her mother had died her grief hadn't manifested itself in overt weeping. Now she knew she was wrong. She had tears a-plenty, and once again it was Thor who had conjured them from the depths of her being.

It was over an hour before she heard the sound of the car returning. Immersed in her thoughts as she'd been, the time had passed quickly, and she hadn't even moved from the edge of the bed.

She'd long since stopped crying, but her eyes were swollen with weeping and tiredness as she raised them wordlessly to Thor's face as he entered the room.

'I'm taking you home now,' he told her curtly. 'Come along.'

Devoid of feeling, walking like an automaton, she followed him downstairs in silence until they turned into the rough road leading towards the farmhouse. To her consternation, Gemma saw it was awash with light. A dreadful premonition brought a pang of fear in its wake. Her eyes dark in her ashen face, she stared at the harsh profile beside her.

'Yes.' Tautly, Thor answered her unspoken question. 'I came to see your lover. I don't believe you know that yesterday he approached me with the purpose of securing a short-term loan in order to keep Tramontana and La Langousta in business. It seems he's been milking their profits to support his jewellery interests.'

'Dear God, it's not true!' But she knew Thor wasn't lying.

He let his eyes linger on her face as he spoke, and for a moment she thought she saw signs of pity in their depths, but it could have been a trick of the light. 'His deadline was noon today.'

'Yes?' She knew what he was going to say. Knew that Josephina and Margarita, Rosa and Leo and the kitchen staff who worked at La Langousta for the evening trade would lose their jobs and she would be to blame, because she'd pierced Thor's pride with the needle of her assumed indifference.

He moved his shoulders in a gesture of rejection. 'How could I do it, Gemma? How could I lend money to a man who cares so little for the woman he's supposed to love that he lends her out like a library book?'

'Noel's not responsible for my actions...' she tried to defend him, but she was so tired, her poor brain so befuddled, this was the final straw. 'So you came and told him he couldn't have the money,' she intoned dully.

'That's right.' He paused, his eyes intently fixed on her pale countenance. 'Instead I made him an offer for his half-share of both businesses and he agreed. We signed a contract which can be legally witnessed in a few hours. Your fiancé has the money which is going to give him a healthy bank balance, and I... I have both catering establishments.'

He was impersonal and businesslike as he continued, his eyes never leaving her troubled face. 'Continuing employment for the existing staff depends entirely on *your* co-operation, Gemma. No!' He held up a hand, pre-empting her protest. 'That's not a form of blackmail, which is what you were going to accuse me of, I'm sure. From what I understand, the efficient running of both concerns depends on your co-ordination with the staff. My wish is merely to ensure the continued profitability of my acquisitions, or I shall have no option but to close them down and put the property to an alternative use. Well?' he asked sharply.

'You have my co-operation,' Gemma whispered.

As Thor leaned across her to open the passenger door, she stumbled out, seeing Noel silhouetted against the light as the front door opened. He held out his arms towards her and, desperately needing the comfort of a true friend, she ran into them, her tired body crumpling against his slender frame as his arms embraced her.

Neither of them turned to watch Thor McCabe's car reverse down the narrow track and turn into the road which would take him back to El Dorado.

CHAPTER EIGHT

'ARE you all right, Gemma?' Noel's question was fraught with concern. 'McCabe told me you'd developed a nasty headache and were lying down and that he'd bring you back when you felt better. Of course, he could have phoned, but he'd reached a decision on some business we'd been discussing and thought he might as well drive over and discuss his proposition with me while you were resting.'

'I'm fine,' she reassured him hollowly, letting him lead her into the house and subsiding weakly into an armchair. 'You've sold out on Tramontana and La Langousta.' Try as she did, she couldn't help the accusing note in her voice.

'Yes.' He lounged down in the chair opposite her, his thin face animated. 'McCabe was right. I was spreading my assets too thinly. I now have a substantial sum in the bank to play with, and Gemma, listen to me. I'm going to give you twenty-five per cent of the sale price!'

'You're what?' She sat bolt upright on the chair, convinced her ears were deceiving her.

Noel grinned at her dazed expression. 'Don't you think you deserve it? For the past five years you've been supervising both places, working for a pittance...'

'But you've paid all the bills,' she protested blankly. 'It's cost me nothing to live here, and there's not much else to spend money on. In fact, I've managed to save quite a bit. Besides, I've enjoyed it immensely.'

'Yes, I know, but it doesn't alter the fact that you were a primary factor in the success we've had, and you deserve to benefit from it! Look, Gemma...' He leaned forward earnestly. 'You have a talent for management, particularly in the catering trade. You owe it to yourself to launch out on your own—go into partnership with a Spanish national, perhaps, as I did, and reap your own rewards.'

'But I'm happy as I am...' Gemma raised dull eyes to his smile. 'I don't have your ambitions. These past years have been therapeutic...'

'You're tired,' he said compassionately. 'And perhaps this isn't the right moment to say it, but isn't it time you finished with therapy? OK, when you first came here you were hurt and bewildered, and the change of scene and climate were just what you needed. But five years, Gem! It's a hell of a long time to fritter away your life. You're intelligent and beautiful—a powerful combination in a woman. It's about time you decided what you really want in the future, and I dare to guess it's more than what you've got at the moment!'

'I don't know what to say...' She was finding it impossible to take in the magnitude of his offer, her mind overburdened with the weight of her jangled emotions. 'Only that it's the most unexpected, generous offer I could ever imagine...'

'And it means you won't have to work for McCabe, either.'

'I...' Gemma hesitated, unwilling to tell Noel of Thor's ultimatum. It would only spoil his pleasure, and she wouldn't want him to guess that it had been intended as a kind of punishment for her attack on his ego. 'Well, I wouldn't want to leave directly,' she compromised. 'Even if I did agree to accept your offer.'

Noel rose abruptly to his feet to stare down at her bent head. 'Look, Gem, you're your own mistress, but I care too much for you as a friend to see you upset. I'd have to be blind not to see that there's still something between you and McCabe. I asked you before and I'm going to ask you again—are you certain that pretending that you and I are going to get married is the wisest thing to do?'

'Yes.' It was little more than a whisper. Noel was right. The period of therapy was over. She dared not regress.

He shrugged his shoulders. 'OK, Gem. But if he's bothering you, just let me know and I'll tell him what he can do with his investment!'

'He may have already decided!' She raised her head to give him a wry smile. 'And he's not bothering me, Noel, I swear it.'

Which was probably the first time she'd perjured herself, she thought listlessly as she dragged her weary body up the stairs. Even Noel's breathtaking offer had failed to act as a balm to her troubled spirit.

Thor arrived at La Langousta the following day, just as they were closing after the lunchtime session. Pleasant and businesslike, he summoned the small staff around him to explain the change of ownership, and to assure them that business would continue as before.

Finding it too painful to watch his handsome, inscrutable face as he mentioned a few improvements he wanted to see made, Gemma allowed her glance to rove round the assembled staff. It was on Josephina that Thor's pep talk was having the most effect, she saw. The Spanish girl's intense gaze was fastened to his face as if every word was a precious pearl. Really, she mused, allowing Thor's lazy drawl to wash over her, Josephina was becoming more striking-looking by the day. Always attractive, with her high-bridged Spanish nose and wide, generous mouth, she seemed to have acquired an additional sparkle and self-confidence recently.

'Gemma?'

Suddenly she was being addressed and was the cynosure of all eyes, and Gemma felt the warm blood of confusion rising to her cheeks.

'Yes?' She met Thor's bland appraisal with a tilt of her chin.

'I was just saying I was relying on you to continue as usual, planning the disposition of staff between the two restaurants, co-ordinating the purchase of food with the chef, keeping a day book and seeing the banking is done promptly.'

'Naturally.' She flashed him a bright smile. 'As well as waiting at table, of course!'

'Of course.' He smiled grimly. 'I shall expect the same co-operation you gave Shelton in all aspects.'

Her dark eyes grew stormy, but she refrained from a retort. She'd made her offer to him—and he'd turned it down. She was no longer prepared to sleep with the boss on any terms, if that was what he was insinuating!

It was the last time she saw him for five days. After the first day, when she experienced only relief, Gemma felt a sense of disappointment at his continued absence. She'd always worked to her utmost ability, but since the changeover she'd made a supreme effort to ensure there would be no justifiable criticism of anything: from the spotless kitchen floor to her own immaculately filed fingernails, she'd insisted on perfection. But Thor didn't come to be impressed.

On the fifth day, after finishing the lunchtime session, she was preparing small vases of fresh flowers ready for the evening tables in the upper restaurant of La Langousta when Josephina called her urgently from the panoramic balcony which encircled it.

'Gemma, come quickly, look at this!'

Joining her, Gemma followed her pointing finger, and let out a low whistle of surprise and admiration.

'It's the *Brisbane Princess*!' Josephina exclaimed excitedly. 'The yacht that Señor McCabe's been expecting. *Madre mía*, but isn't she a beauty?'

She was too, Gemma agreed silently. In a port which hosted the luxurious craft of international millionaires, the sparkling white motor yacht proceeding up to the berths outside the Mahón Yacht Club was well able to hold her own. So this was Thor's partner. She bit her lip contemplatively, well aware of how much it would cost to own and run a vessel of that size and structure. If its owner agreed to invest in Parangas, it seemed Noel's future would be very rosy.

As the craft moved majestically past their grandstand viewpoint, her raised sun-deck became visible, and Josephina placed her hand on Gemma's arm.

'Look—do you suppose that's the owner's wife?'

The woman stretched out on her back beneath the hot fingers of the early afternoon sun wore a minuscule bikini. Long limbs tanned a deep bronze were a fabulous contrast to the ultra-white scraps of material which trisected her curvaceous body; white-blonde hair spread like a curtain on the dark covered air bed beneath her. It was impossible at that distance to see her face, only the dark glasses that protected her vision from the molten heat beating down from the cloudless sky, but she was young and almost certainly beautiful. A millionaire's wife—or a millionaire's daughter? For a reason she didn't even want to examine, Gemma found herself wanting to believe it was the former.

'He probably named the yacht after her,' Josephina enthused. 'She looks like the Princesses in the Hans Andersen stories.'

'Very probably,' Gemma returned curtly. 'Have you finished what you were doing?' She was angry with herself when Josephina cast her a hurt look before turning away from the scene and re-entering the restaurant without comment.

Damn! She ran her fingers through her hair. She'd never spoken in such a peremptory tone to any of the staff before, and Josephina was a friend as well as a colleague. What was the matter with her? Nothing, she decided hardily, that Thor's imminent departure wouldn't cure! A few more days and a decision would have been reached. For Noel's sake she hoped it was favourable to his plans; for her own part she didn't care. As long as the tall Australian departed from her life and allowed her to repair the damage his sudden reappearance had caused to her peace of mind, she'd be contented!

It was nine-thirty the same evening when Thor strolled into the upstairs restaurant at La Langousta, accompanied by a middle-aged couple and the young woman Gemma had already termed in her mind the 'Brisbane Princess'. Standing behind the glass windowed doors leading to the kitchen, Gemma watched the small party with interest, as Thor chose one of the few remaining vacant tables, pulling out a chair for the blonde with an air of old-world courtesy.

The man had to be Edmund Curran and the woman seated next to him his wife, Gemma decided, seeing the way the couple looked at each other and catching the man's deep Australian twang. That left the Brisbane Princess as their daughter, since there was a remarked similarity between the two women, except that where the elder was elegant and well-groomed, the younger was outstandingly pretty.

A small twinge of what could only be jealousy twisted Gemma's heart, as she watched Thor lean towards the curvaceous blonde, sharing the menu, his head only inches away from the warm thrust of golden, vol-

uptuous breasts that appeared to be bursting forth from
the white figure-hugging dress she wore.

Why did he have to bring them here? Did he want to
flaunt Curran's daughter in her face—a living proof that
she, Gemma, wasn't the only fish in the sea as far as he
was concerned? As if she had ever doubted that!

Dear heavens, what was happening to her? Gemma
relaxed her clenched fingers. She was behaving as if she
were still the unsophisticated teenager who thought
Thor's passionate words gave her some claim to his
loyalty. And, apart from her emotional illogicality, she
was also being unreasonable in a practical sense. With
Rosa improving by the day, but not yet discharged from
the hospital, Josephina could hardly be spared in the
evening to do outside catering, and after all, Thor part-
owned the restaurant! Of course it was inevitable he'd
bring his friends here to dine. She just wished she'd
foreseen the eventuality earlier and been more prepared
for it.

For a moment she contemplated asking Margarita to
take over her service at the table, then discarded the
notion. She wasn't that much of a coward. True, her
last personal encounter with Thor McCabe had ended
in disaster, but she wouldn't allow that to spoil her
professional approach!

Glancing into the small mirror beside the door, she
checked her appearance. Because of the heat in the
kitchen she wore little make-up, but her tanned skin was
smooth and unblemished, her naturally dark eyebrows
winging cleanly over her thickly lashed dark eyes. Only
her lips owed something to art, scarlet and dewy with
lip gloss. She'd enhanced their natural luscious curves
to match the scarlet dress she'd chosen to wear: a fine
Spanish cotton, the bodice stitched on one shoulder but
falling to beneath the armpit on the other, leaving one
golden shoulder bare. Fitted to the waist, it skimmed

over her hips to widen into a flare on the knee, allowing her to walk with elegance and ease.

Nothing remarkable, but she'd pass muster, she allowed critically, about to walk out into the restaurant when her eye alighted on a single hibiscus bloom which one of the evening staff must have found lying on the patio. Its colour echoed exactly the scarlet of her dress. In what was almost an act of defiance Gemma picked it up and tucked it into her hair, fastening it so it lay between her neck and one bare shoulder.

As she approached Thor's table, a cold hand seemed to clutch at her heart as he raised his eyes, meeting her professional smile of welcome with a blank gaze. So he didn't even want to recognise her socially now he was with his wealthy friends, she observed grimly, as it was left to Edmund Curran to give her a friendly grin.

Standing ramrod-stiff, she waited in silence, as the party argued in a friendly fashion among themselves as to what they would have, leaving it to Thor to place the final choice on their behalf. He gave the order in his lazy drawl, never by a flicker of an eyelid indicating that he had any knowledge of her existence outside the confines of the restaurant.

Returning to the kitchen, aware of the light-hearted laughter following in her wake, Gemma chided herself for her reaction. She'd insulted Thor's odd sense of honour and he'd finally decided to abandon any attempt to take advantage of their earlier relationship. It was what she wanted! It was absurd to feel slighted.

But as the evening wore on, to her own annoyance, Gemma's sense of desolation increased. The 'Brisbane Princess' was all over Thor. With her blonde hair tossing, she seemed to dominate the small party, but most of her attention was for the man sitting beside her. Her long, slim arm festooning his shoulder or encircling his waist, her pale blue eyes flirting with him or commanding his attention, her pretty mouth pouting up at him, she left little doubt to any onlooker as to where her interest lay. And all the time her slightly high-pitched nasal voice echoed above the muted sounds from the other diners, until Gemma thought she'd scream if she heard her say 'Thor, darling' one more time.

It was nearly midnight when she presented the bill to Thor, watching impassively as he wrote his signature on the back of it.

'That was an excellent meal—well served.' He reached into his trouser pocket, pulling out a handful of *peseta* notes, choosing two and offering them to her. 'Here, this is for you.'

Drawing in her breath with a hiss of displeasure, Gemma met his bland appraisal. It was ridiculous to feel insulted—but she did. The value of the tip was well above what any waitress might reasonably have expected, and that alone made it suspect. What was he trying to do? Show off in front of his wealthy friends, impress the 'Brisbane Princess' with his largesse? Or was he making some personal point, a token show of paying for her company the last time, with a few hundred *pesetas*? Her mind in a whirl, her heart thudding in wordless protest, Gemma stared at the proffered notes. If he'd felt obliged to leave a tip, then he could have put it discreetly on the table and it would have gone into the pool for the other staff. She never doubted for a moment that the way he'd chosen to present it to her had been calculated as a deliberate slight.

She hesitated, seeing a bright challenge in the blue eyes that met her own as if they'd pierce into her skull. To refuse, to acknowledge that she resented his attitude, would not only seem strange to his companions, it would also deprive the kitchen staff of a well-deserved bonus. She reached out slim fingers, taking the notes from his hand.

'Gracias, Señor.' She smiled sweetly, almost coquettishly. 'I'm so glad you enjoyed it. I do hope we have the pleasure of your company again in the near future.'

'Oh, you will.' The assurance came double quick as the others rose from their seats, his voice deepening to a harsh whisper unheard by any save herself, 'And probably much sooner than you think!'

It was mid-afternoon the following day before she realised the terse promise had been more than a glib retort. Lunch time at La Langousta had been busy, the attractive outside courtyard with its view of the magnificent harbour drawing in the growing crowds of holidaymakers in increasing numbers. If Thor had really intended carrying out his threat of changing the usage of the two restaurants, he would have surely cut off his own nose to spite his face, Gemma decided grimly, wondering if his threat had been as sincere as she'd first supposed. Well, since she'd no wish to put her suspicion to the test, she supposed she'd never find out!

Bending to her task of cleaning down the food preparation surface in the streamlined kitchen, she heard the sound of the swing doors opening behind her.

'Oh, have you finished with those plates already, Josephina? That was quick!' She turned round, pushing a fallen lock of hair away from her damp forehead.

'Thor!' His name burst from her lips before she could control them. 'What are *you* doing here?'

He gave her a quizzical look. 'What do you suppose? Checking up on my assets, of course.' He smiled carelessly into her guarded eyes.

'Of course,' she accorded pleasantly. 'I trust everything is proceeding to your satisfaction?'

'Well, there's no problem with the restaurants,' he agreed, pulling out a chair from its position against the wall and swinging it round to face him before seating himself astride, arms akimbo on its back, all the time watching her with enigmatic eyes. 'In fact, they're the least of my worries.'

'Parangas, then?' Her pulse quickened, as a feeling close to despair surged through her. 'Your friend Curran doesn't like it?'

'On the contrary, he's most interested.' Thor stretched out his jean-clad legs with a nonchalant grace. 'As a matter of fact we're having a meeting tonight to discuss a few minor alterations to the plans, after which I anticipate we'll be approaching your boyfriend and his partner with a concrete proposition.'

'But that's marvellous!' Excitement made Gemma's eyes sparkle. 'Oh, I wish I could let Noel know, but he left for Barcelona this morning...' She broke off as she saw his lips twist into a cynical curve, adding more quietly, 'Thank you for letting me know, Thor. It's a great weight off my mind.'

'I don't doubt it, in view of your pending marriage.' He swept a critical glance over her as she stiffened beneath his appraisal, suddenly conscious of the sight she must look, her pale lemon slacks and matching top wrapped round in a protective overall. Sensing his supercilious amusement, she unbuttoned the latter, shrugging it away from her shoulders, to be rewarded with an appreciative gleam in his expression.

She was a fool to let his opinion influence her, she thought bitterly, taking a few steps to hang the overall in a cupboard, tensely aware of his brooding presence: of the black T-shirt clinging lovingly to the well-defined pectoral ridge across his chest; the long, muscled legs astride the chair. Thor was a superb specimen of *homo sapiens*, she conceded, with his powerful shoulders, trim waist and lean hips; but one couldn't judge a man on appearance alone...

'How's the "Bris..."' she began, catching herself just in time. 'I mean how's Mr Curran's daughter—I assume it was his daughter with him last night? She seemed to be enjoying herself.'

'Jealous, Gemma?' His lip curled derisively as he rose to his feet and narrowed the distance between them. 'You needn't be. Eloise is a pretty girl, but she means as little to me now as she did a couple of years ago when I first set eyes on her.'

'Really? How interesting.' Gemma struggled to cling to her pride. 'But I'm not concerned with your emotional involvements.'

'Then perhaps you should be!' He rammed his hands in his pockets and glared down at her. 'Because the only involvement I want is with you. Be honest with me, Gemma. Didn't you enjoy the time we've spent together these last few days?'

She stared back at him, blindingly aware that it was true. 'But you asked me to show you round the island,' she protested at last.

'Yes, I did,' he acknowledged impatiently. 'Now I'm asking you if you enjoyed it.' His tone demanded an answer.

'It's not a fair question. Of course I enjoyed myself.' She lifted her dark head and met his intense regard with a sparkling challenge of her own. 'Who wouldn't have a good time in a lovely place like this?'

The blue eyes sharpened at her retort. 'I'm not talking about Menorca and well you know it! I'm talking about sharing: sitting on a beach, watching fireworks, eating lobster... I'm talking about the garden of Golden Farm, the hallway in Ciudadela, the bedroom at Sabina...' He held her eyes with deliberate intent in the heady silence which followed. 'I'm talking about what happened between us, Gemma.'

'Nothing happened!' she declared stormily, lowering her eyes before he could see the embarrassed colour that heated her cheeks.

'Nothing?' A soft smile touched Thor's sensuous mouth. 'Oh, Gemma...my poor, beautiful Gemma, you may be able to fool yourself, but you can't fool me. You can't go on running away from the past as you fled from the horses at the fiesta. Is *this* nothing...?'

'Don't touch me!' She sprang away from his reaching arms, her nerves stretched to breaking point, determined to resist the purpose she read on his lean face. She mustn't allow him to call her bluff. Never, ever again would she allow him to possess her. She had teetered on the brink that night at Sabina. By a miracle she had survived and she was grateful for it! No man, let alone Thor McCabe, was worth the enduring agony of loving and losing.

'Are you afraid of me?' To her gratification, he'd frozen at her harsh command, but it had done nothing to strip his attitude of arrogance, she recognised despairingly.

'No,' she lied. Afraid? Of course she was afraid, terrified that with a little more perseverance he'd break through her reserve once more and turn her into the weak, fawning idolatress she'd once been. With an effort she managed to regain her composure. 'Can't you understand, Thor—I don't want to resurrect the past?'

'Gemma...please...' His voice was deeply persuasive. 'Don't shut me out. I know I've given you reason to see me as ruthless and unprincipled, but all that's changed. I swear it. Give me another chance to show you how much you mean to me...'

But for how long—a week, a month? At his words, Gemma's eyes closed momentarily in a brave effort to keep back her tears. But she couldn't entirely mask the way her voice shook as she whispered, 'It's too late, Thor. My future is already planned and it doesn't include you. You know how things are between me and Noel.'

'Do I?' He laughed harshly, ignoring the plea for clemency her dark eyes begged. 'I'm beginning to wonder. Look, Gemma—the last thing I want to do is hurt you again. If I really believed you were in love with Noel Shelton, then I'd turn my back on my own desires and go out of your life for ever. But whatever it is you and Noel have, it's not a patch on what you and I once shared—and you know it as well as I do!' He stared down at her, his face set and unfathomable, waiting for her answer, and it was as much as she could do to trust herself to speak.

'How dare you?' she gasped, furious at his perspicacity. By attacking the veil of deception she'd rigged for her own protection, he was stripping away the only positive defence she had against him. She couldn't have felt more outraged if he'd shredded her clothes, leaving her naked and exposed to a cruel world. 'Once, you and I might have had something going for us. Once! But never again!' She sucked in her breath, glaring at him, panting and flushed. 'Can't you get it into your head that I want you to go away and leave me alone? You lost any right to interfere in my life five years ago. What I do now is my own affair.'

'But that's just it. It's not the kind of affair you want me to believe, is it?' Stubbornly, he laboured his point. 'For God's sake, Gemma, I've held you in my arms, kissed you, felt your response. No...' He seized her shoulders with rough hands as she would have moved away. 'Don't turn your back on me. You know every word I've spoken is the truth. The engagement ring that sat so strangely on your finger—it wasn't even yours, was it? Here...' He released one of her shoulders to delve in his pocket, producing Stella's solitaire. 'You left it behind at the villa, and you haven't even missed it, have you?' He slammed it down on the adjacent work surface. 'Have you?' he demanded inexorably.

She was shattered and unable to hide it, hating the
cruel satisfaction she read on his face. Everything he'd
said was true! But she'd die rather than admit it. It hadn't
been what he'd done to her all that time ago—it had
been the manner of it ... It was impossible to believe he
was thinking of anyone else but himself now—as he
always did. She wouldn't be made a fool of twice.

'I...' She looked defiantly into Thor's lean, angry face,
saw a hard muscle jerking spasmodically in his jaw, his
eyes bright and dangerous beneath lowered lids, and
couldn't find the words she wanted to deny his
supposition.

Before she had a chance to gather her thoughts it was
too late. With a muffled exclamation Thor pulled her
into his arms, taking her lips in the familiar, intimate
way that went on and on and left her breathless and
shaking when at last he lifted his head away and looked
down at her. Their bodies were still in intimate contact;
the light summer clothing between them might never have
existed as their body heat mingled.

'Gemma...' It was a husky caress as Thor raised one
hand to the back of her head, threading his fingers
through the lush softness of her dark hair, pushing her
back hard against the wall so that she could feel the
strength of his lean, muscular thighs. Held prisoner, not
strong enough to oppose his sleek body with its finely
tuned muscles, Gemma had no means of combating him,
as his other hand moved to her breast to caress its ripe
fullness with gentle, loving fingers.

She moaned as eagerly they wrought the magic she'd
dreaded to experience—the liquid warmth welling inside
her, as the yawning desire for physical fulfilment with
the man she'd never stopped loving flooded through her.
Another moment and she'd be reaching to touch the
shallow curves of his hard, masculine body, the narrow
pelvis, the strong hips, the hollow flanks that pro-

claimed his fitness and his youth... Another moment
and she would be lost, pouring out the words he wanted
to hear...

'I want you, Gemma. I've never wanted anyone the
way I wanted you. What I did to you was unavoidable
at the time and no one regrets it more than me, but is
it really impossible for us to start again where we left
off?'

'Thor...I...' She faltered as the sound of the swing
doors opening broke through the lethargy of passion
Thor's ardency had engendered. Josephina! Dear
heavens, she'd forgotten the Spanish girl hadn't yet left.
As Thor, too, became aware of the disturbance, stepping
back in surprise, Gemma managed to slip away from his
grasp, walking quickly towards the centre of the room
as Josephina, having glimpsed the intimacy of their previous embrace, made a silent and speedy withdrawal.

Another second and she would have committed
herself! Gemma's mind reeled as she acknowledged how
close she'd been to confessing her love. Now circumstances, fate, call it what you would, had given her yet
another chance to keep her self-respect.

Hands that trembled reached for the sparkling
diamond before her. Deliberately she slid it on to her
ring finger before raising a look devoid of all emotion
to the man who approached her with quick strides.

She'd learned to live without him before. She could
learn again. 'You're becoming a megalomaniac, Thor,'
she told him coldly. 'Just because I exchanged a few
kisses with you for old times' sake, it doesn't mean you
have any place in my present life. Noel and I are very
much in love and have every intention of getting married
this autumn in England.'

His face became a mask, but she could see the pulse
hammering away on his neck beneath his ear, and she

fancied that behind the set jaw he'd clenched his teeth to keep control of himself.

'And if I were to tell you there was a very good reason why I went back to Australia so suddenly, that it had nothing to do with chasing cattle or making my fortune, and that at the time I had no other option but to appear the rogue you still see me as ... If I were to tell you *that*, Gemma, would it make any difference at all to your plans?'

How could it? she questioned herself wearily. There was no possible excuse that would absolve him from shattering her life with such callousness, although she didn't doubt his mind was agile enough and his tongue smooth enough to invent some story that would touch her now her defences were so low.

She swallowed, gathering her resolve. 'No difference,' she averred coolly. 'Noel and I are in love. That's all there is to it.'

'I see.' Thor nodded gravely. 'Then I'll accept that as your final statement and leave you in peace. I wish the both of you the best of luck. Just one last thing, though ...' Before she realised his intention, he'd taken her right hand. Lifting it to his mouth with palm open, he placed a soft, dry kiss in its warm, sensitive centre, folding her fingers over, as if to hold it captive. 'If you ever change your mind, come to me, Gemma and let me know. Anywhere, any time ... I'll be waiting.'

Before she could react, he'd released her hand and was striding out of the swing doors without a backwards look, leaving Gemma standing alone, her clenched fist pressed hard against her heart.

Suddenly spurred to action, she raced out of the kitchen, across the deserted dining-room, and gazed down at the patio as Thor appeared, walking with a fast, measured stride. She watched him until he'd passed from view, before opening her hand and staring down at the empty palm while scalding tears fell unheeded down her cheeks.

CHAPTER NINE

BY LATE afternoon the same day the weather had changed. Riding back to the farmhouse on her motor scooter, Gemma had noticed the thickening clouds and felt the first gusts of wind teasing her hair. Could it be they were in for a brief visit from the notorious *tramontana*? she wondered—the brutal wind after which Noel's bar had been named. It would certainly account for her feeling of enervation and depression!

She'd lived in Menorca long enough to know that the harsh wind which gusted down from the high mountains of Russia in the winter, sweeping everything before it, licking the sand on the beaches into dunes, shredding the straw beach umbrellas, and sucking the oxygen out of the air, was an occasional unwelcome visitor to the island. Although fortunately in the holiday season it rarely lasted more than a day, the high temperatures returning immediately on its departure.

By early evening she knew her supposition had been correct. Opening the front door carefully, she stepped outside. The force of the wind against her face was as strong as a restraining hand, whipping her hair into a frenzy and tearing at the loose cotton top she was wearing.

Well, she decided dourly, there was certainly no possibility of putting the usual tables and chairs outside the bar, but there might be a few hardy tourists who would enjoy pitting their strength against the wind, so she'd go there anyway. At least the small bar inside would be cosy for any intrepid traveller!

Dressing herself suitably in denim jeans topped with a long-sleeved cotton sweater and a nylon windcheater, she couldn't help wishing Noel wasn't in Barcelona. It was only a short visit to see Ramón Casados and their bank manager, and she expected him back the next day—but at that moment she'd willingly have swopped her light motor scooter for the security of Noel's old car! Still, she would take particular care, knowing full well how the wind could lift the small bike and pitch it across the road even at relatively low speeds.

Half an hour later she was breathing a sigh of relief as she rode carefully down the steep slope to the small, rocky inlet. Here, at least, the steep cliffs offered protection. How desolate Tramontana looked! Its sun umbrellas battened down, its tables stacked against a wall where Leo had left them after lunch, the sun-blind securely furled and fastened.

Once inside, she inspected the fridge and found everything in order. Hopefully Leo would put in an appearance soon, and she'd have someone to talk to. Then, after a couple of hours, if no customers ventured in, she'd close down and have an early night for a change.

She was reaching for a tin of instant coffee, having decided to make herself a drink, when the door burst open and Leo precipitated himself into the room.

'Leo! For God's sake, what's the matter?' It had only taken one look at his face to know that something was drastically wrong.

'Josephina...it's Josephina. She's going to kill herself!'

A terrible coldness invaded Gemma's limbs as she stared at the young Spaniard's white face, temporarily bereft of speech.

'She is, she is, Gemma!' he reiterated his allegation, black eyes fastened to her astounded countenance. 'For pity's sake, help me!'

'Yes, of course I will, Leo.' Instantly she offered her aid. 'But where is she? What's happened?'

'Thor McCabe is what's happened!' His mouth worked with bitter emotion as Gemma felt a growing nausea spread its fingers through her body. 'He dishonoured her, robbed her of her virtue, promised he'd marry her...'

'Oh, no!' It was little more than a whisper as Gemma grabbed at the edge of the bar for support. Not again! Dear God, not again! What he'd done to her had been bad enough, but to Josephina... An employee, a Spanish girl whose family lived by the age-old rules of the Catholic Church...chastity and continence! How right she'd been not to trust him, and how sick the realisation of that fact made her feel!

'It's true.' She saw accusation a bright flame on his strained face. 'Then today at Langousta she saw the two of you together...'

Furiously Gemma fought the wave of faintness that darkened the dim-lit interior still further. Yes, Josephina had been there. She'd opened the door just as Thor was saying that he wanted her, Gemma, and was begging her to say she reciprocated his feeling. They'd been moulded together, their bodies intimately locked... All the time he'd been trying to make her believe he'd returned to Menorca just to see her again he'd been seducing her Spanish friend! But this was no time to concentrate on her own agony.

Yet some last remnant of faith, some desperate flicker of hope, forced her to ask the question.

'Leo, are you sure?'

'My sister's no liar!' The proud retort admonished her. 'I found her at home this afternoon when I'd closed down here. Lying on the floor, sobbing and sobbing. She told me everything. How she'd seen you and McCabe at Langousta by accident and had unwittingly overheard your conversation.' His bitter tone condemned her. 'She kept crying over and over again—"He promised he'd marry me...he promised there was only me. I loved him... I gave myself to him...he said I'd be his wife..."'

'Poor little Josephina...' Gemma's voice broke on a sob.

'She was distraught, hysterical!' Leo punished Gemma with his harsh account. 'She kept crying out that she should never have worked for him, never listened to his lies. So I told her I'd *make* him marry her...' His chin thrust upwards with all the bravado of his race as Gemma felt her heart sink even lower. No one would make Thor McCabe do anything against his will. In his creed, there were no old-world standards of honour and decency.

'She wouldn't listen to me. She said he loved you...'

Gemma licked parched lips, dredging her voice from her constricted throat. 'No, he doesn't, Leo, and I don't love him. Is that what you want me to tell your sister?'

'If she's still alive, it might help. You see, she's gone. Taken my motor scooter and gone. She left a note saying she was going to jump from the cliffs like Xuroy.'

Whatever energy she had left seemed to drain from Gemma's slender body as she pictured the Menorcan girl, sick with fear and shame after seeing the man she loved, the man she'd allowed to love her, whispering endearments to another girl. She'd seen what being in love had done to Josephina, knew the joy she must have felt even to allow Thor to touch her intimately, let alone love her completely, witnessed the incandescent glow of love on the girl's face. Yes, she thought bitterly, when a woman has loved like that, death is a very real alternative to desertion.

'We have to get to her!' Leo's desperate voice reached through the dark caverns of Gemma's mind. 'But I've got no transport. Can we follow her on your scooter?'

'I have a better idea.' Gemma's basic courage was coming to her aid as she strove to resolve the emergency. 'Thor McCabe's responsible for what's happened—he can deal with it. We'll go on my scooter to El Dorado. It's much nearer than the caves anyway, and *he* can drive us there.'

As relief surged through Leo's taut features, Gemma locked up the bar. Seconds later she was riding pillion, her arms wound tightly round the lithe young body of the Menorcan boy, her cheek pressed against his back. Leo had insisted on driving and she'd had no heart to argue. He was going much too fast, she registered, as the sand from the road stung her face and her eyes became sore from the grit which penetrated her lowered lashes, but she couldn't protest in the circumstances, and at least she had an excuse for the tears which streamed down her face from her swollen eye-ducts.

Thor had proved himself beyond doubt as being unscrupulous, as she'd always thought. Instead of the triumph she should have felt at the accuracy of her diagnosis, she felt only a deep, devastating misery.

It was something of a miracle, she admitted with a heartfelt prayer of gratitude, when they arrived at their destination uninjured and she could see the lights on in the Villa Sabina through the half-shuttered windows.

'Stay here,' she directed Leo. 'I'll get him.'

'No,' he opposed her harshly. 'She's my sister—it should be me——'

'Don't forget, I'm involved as well,' Gemma retorted coldly, drawing on her resources to give a note of authority to her instruction. 'Wait here for me.'

She slipped off the back of the scooter before he could protest further and ran to the door of the villa. She'd been afraid that Leo would lash out at Thor the moment he saw him—probably with a knife in his hand—and she'd been afraid. Not on Thor's account, the heartless

Australian had asked for everything he got, but on Leo's because he was much slighter than the older man. Besides, any delay could be fatal. Her one ray of hope was that Josephina had said where she was going. It made her gesture sound like a cry for help. Gemma prayed she'd wait for that help to arrive.

Jamming her finger against the doorbell, she kept it there for the few seconds it took Thor to answer it.

'Dear God! Gemma!' He stared aghast at her disfigured face. 'What's happened, sweetheart?'

The endearment, spoken in his husky drawl, was the last straw. Violently she shouldered her way past him as he went to draw her across the threshold. In the gracious sitting-room, the Currans turned astonished eyes on the windblown apparition she made.

'Happened?' Her voice was clear and carrying, pitched artificially high as Thor followed her and she turned to look at him, scorn etched on every taut line of her lovely face. What did she care now for the munificence of his friends? Let them see him as the rotter he undoubtedly was, and if Parangas was the price of her revenge—then so be it. Josephina was worth more than a heap of steel and concrete!

'What's happened, Mr McCabe, is that the little Spanish girl you made your mistress overheard you this morning trying to persuade me to follow her example, and, not realising you make a hobby of that kind of thing, she took it to mean you no longer intended to marry her as you'd promised.' She heaved in a deep breath, ignoring both the blank astonishment that froze his countenance, and the amazed reaction from his guests. 'Yes, Mr McCabe,' she told him brutally, 'your Josephina is on her way to jump off the cliffs at the caves of Xuroy.'

'How did you get here?' The terse response took her by surprise as Thor grabbed her arm. Somehow she'd expected a downright denial, a disclaimer of responsibility.

'With Leo. On my scooter.'

'You might both have been killed in this weather.' His tone was as forbidding as the hard lines of his face. 'I'll get my car out. How long ago did she leave, and what transport did she have?'

'Not long ago, I think.' She was confused. 'You'll have to ask Leo. He came directly to me when he read her note. And she took his motor scooter.'

'Then we must pray we can overtake her before she gets to the caves—or has an accident.' He turned briefly towards the Currans. 'I'm sorry, but this is an emergency, as you can see. I'll explain to you when I get back.'

He didn't wait for their murmurs of acceptance as he pushed Gemma towards the front door with scant ceremony. 'Move, Gemma. We can't afford to waste any time.'

Gemma obeyed. Thor's calmness, his air of authority, his willing acceptance of his implication in the affair, had lifted a load from her shoulders.

It was while he was unlocking the car door that Leo abandoned the scooter, racing forward to lunge a blow at Thor's face. With a muttered curse the Australian rolled away from the attack, grabbing Leo's arm and twisting it up behind his back. As Leo yelled in pain and frustration, Gemma seized Thor's free arm, digging her fingers into the firm muscle.

'Leave him alone!' she yelled. 'Don't you think you've done enough harm?'

'And let him hit me?' Thor's sarcasm stung like a whiplash. 'Now, listen to me, both of you. The important thing is to find Josephina. Until then, I don't want to discuss the matter at all.'

'But *I* do!' Leo's fiery Spanish pride flared as Thor released his hold.

Thor swore succinctly at the other man. 'If it's going to make you any happier, then I promise you that if Josephina wants me to marry her I will!'

Gemma gasped as Leo grunted, apparently content with Thor's guarantee. Climbing into the back seat of the car with Leo, she felt as if she'd been flayed with rawhide, every bone in her body aching. She should have felt overjoyed for Josephina at Thor's unexpected declaration. All she did feel was a great, empty desolation.

No one spoke as Thor concentrated on what he was doing. All watched the dark, lonely road for the sight of the young girl on the motor scooter, but it remained obdurately empty. They passed no one.

Running down the steep steps cut into the cliff, behind the two men, the wind buffeting her against the craggy sides, Gemma felt the supporting rail on her other side shift dangerously, a fragile barrier between herself and the churning, wild sea whipped to a frenzy some sixty meters below. And if Josephina wasn't here? Dear God, what then? she prayed.

But she was. Beyond the entrance to the caves themselves, the cliff ballooned out above the sea, forming a natural viewing platform. Here, in fine weather, there were once tables and chairs of the nightclub. Tonight, the platform was devoid of life save for one small figure.

Her narrow skirt plastered against her legs by the violence of the wind, her long hair streaming back from her face, nothing between her and a plummeting drop of more than a hundred and fifty feet except a rustic rail that moved visibly beneath her clutching hands, stood Josephina.

In front of her Gemma heard Leo cry out, saw him try and push his way past Thor, only to be restrained.

'No,' the older man commanded sharply. 'Let *me* go to her.'

Leo hesitated for a second, then stopped as Thor went forward alone. Gemma watched, her heart in her mouth, as he braced himself against the wind which threatened to pluck him from his narrow perch at every step.

There was only a fitful light from a transient moon, but Thor's pale shirt reflected what light was available. Suddenly it seemed that the Menorcan girl realised she was no longer alone, for she edged her way to the furthest corner of her perilous sanctuary. Thor called something out to her, but his voice was tossed away by the wind. In an agony of suspense, Gemma reached for Leo and felt the young man's arm tighten round her shoulders, as Thor approached the pitiful figure of his sister, both terrified that she might pitch herself on to the jagged rocks that lay waiting like angry teeth to receive her.

Then abruptly it was over, as Thor reached the platform and took Josephina into his arms, pinioning her safely to his own strong body.

'Why doesn't he bring her back?' Leo was aggressively angry, impatient that the two figures should stand exposed and vulnerable against such a dangerous backdrop.

'Let him talk to her first,' Gemma said quietly. 'He has to talk to her alone, Leo.'

It seemed a lifetime, but it couldn't have been more than a couple of minutes before Thor led Josephina away from the edge of the cliffs to the comparative safety of the path.

'Josephina!' Leo took her unresisting body from Thor's arm. 'How could you——'

'I must talk to you, Leo.' Ashen-faced, her eyes dark pools in her drawn face, Josephina refused to let him finish his sentence. 'You have to know...'

'Not now!' It was Thor who interrupted with terse determination. 'No explanations until we get out of this wretched wind and somewhere civilised.' He turned to Gemma. 'Can we go back to the farmhouse?'

'Yes, of course.' It was the obvious choice. As Thor had said, there were explanations to be made, and there would be no place for them in Josephina's crowded home. The Villa Sabina was the other side of Mahón. The farmhouse was ideal, and as soon as they got there Leo could phone his mother and tell her his sister was safe.

Sitting beside Thor on the journey, Gemma glanced at his unsmiling profile. Had he really meant what he'd said about marrying the Spanish girl? How tired and drawn he looked, the skin stretched tautly across his fine cheek bones, the familiar scar a white slash against his tan, the first hint of dark shadow round his pale lips and firm chin. She could almost find it in her heart to be sorry for him. Whatever he'd done, he'd behaved impeccably since the moment she'd asked his help; but it was only when they reached the farmhouse that Thor would really show his measure as a man.

Stepping into the main living-room, Josephina turned beseechingly to Gemma. 'Please, I must speak to my brother alone.'

'Josephina—I . . .'

'No!' It was Thor, his interruption unduly sharp. 'Let her speak to Leo.'

Turning to protest at his arbitrary instruction, Gemma paused, seeing something in the set of his jaw that restrained her.

'I—I'll tidy myself up, then,' she said briefly, accepting his request without further contention.

Upstairs, the mirror in her bedroom confirmed her worst fears. Stoically she disciplined herself to wash the dirt from her face and brush the tangles from her hair. There was no hiding the ravages of tears and wind, but at least she was clean.

'Gemma?'

She started at Thor's soft voice outside the door. 'I've brought you a drink. May I come in?'

'There's no point.' She opened the door to find him standing on the threshold, a glass in each hand.

'Scotch,' he told her tersely, following her gaze. 'I'm afraid I helped myself. I think you may need it.'

'Thank you, but——'

'No buts, Gemma. There are things I have to tell you.' Ignoring her feeble attempt to keep him out, Thor entered the small bedroom, swinging a chair round as he'd done in La Langousta earlier and seating himself astride it.

'Sit down,' he invited her kindly, nodding to the single bed and handing her one of the glasses. 'You've got to hear me out.'

'I know everything I need to know.' But she took the glass, sinking down on the bed and taking a sip from it before meeting his blue stare. 'You don't need to explain anything to me. I understand.' She swallowed, too proud for recriminations. 'Josephina's a lovely girl and she's obviously very much in love with you.'

'Not *me*, Gemma.' The words held a kind of sadness as the blue eyes clouded with compassion.

'Of course *you*!' How dared he deny it? 'She told Leo. She saw you and me together this afternoon. That's what upset her. That's why she——'

'It's not what she *saw*. It's what she *heard*.'

She stared at him. He'd never been so distanced from her, yet she had a strange compulsion to reach out her hand and push the wind tousled hair back from his broad forehead, to feel the roughness of his cheek in her palm. These were the thoughts of madness!

'Heard?' She took another sip of Scotch. 'Yes, she heard you say you wanted me.' It was impossible to look at him as she said the words.

'Not what *I* said—what *you* said,' he insisted softly.

Now Gemma did look up. 'I didn't say anything,' she retorted fiercely. 'You know I didn't. In fact, I told you I was going to marry——' Her voice tailed off. She felt her jaw gape and knew she was sitting there like a zombie, unable to think, let alone speak. As if in a nightmare, she saw Thor's face swim before her, saw him nod towards the glass in her hand. Obediently she raised it to her lips and swallowed its fiery contents.

'I'm sorry, Gemma. So terribly sorry.' His handsome face was still, the eyes guarded. 'There wasn't an easy way to tell you.'

'Noel?' The name was a hoarse whisper. '*Noel* is her lover?'

The tawny, gold-shot head dipped in silent acquiescence.

'But—but she told Leo it was *you*! She said she'd seen you and me together!'

'She was incoherent. Yes, she told him about seeing and hearing us, but she kept repeating—"he said he would marry me." Don't you see, when she heard you say you and Noel were going to be married this year, she thought—still thinks—that he lied to her...and then, of course, there was the ring she saw you put on your finger. She was outside the doors, not meaning to eavesdrop, waiting for us to go so she could finish her work. When she sobbed out how she'd been betrayed, *she* knew she meant Noel. But her words were so disjointed that Leo misunderstood.'

'And you knew the truth all the time? Even when I came to you and told you what had happened...oh, no!' Remembering how she'd burst into his house and insulted him in front of the Currans, she put her empty glass down on the bedside table and buried her face in her hands, rocking backwards and forwards in misery and embarrassment. 'What must you have thought?'

'That you badly needed help.' He spoke with a wry humour, not the contempt she'd expected or deserved. 'And, yes, I guessed the truth. Well,' Gemma lifted her head to see a slight smile turn the corners of his mouth, 'I knew it wasn't me. The only other person who fitted the bill was Noel.'

'Oh, poor Josephina!' Gemma winced at what her own selfishness had inflicted on her friend.

'Yes, poor Josephina, indeed.' Thor rose to his feet, downed his own drink and walked across to the window, pulling a gap in the Venetian blinds and gazing out into nothingness, as Gemma tried to reassemble her thoughts.

'So what did you say to her at the caves?' she asked at last, surprised to find she could control the quaver in her voice.

'What could I say?' Thor shrugged. 'I told her that Leo had misunderstood her and that she must come back and tell him the truth. I told her she must wait for Noel to return from Barcelona and face him with her doubts, and finally I told her that love—like most things in this life—has its price... but that price is seldom death.'

'I see.' Gemma swallowed to ease a throat stinging from raw spirit. 'So now she's telling Leo the full story.'

Thor didn't answer. Looking at the tensed muscles of his back, Gemma realised what an ordeal he'd gone through. Perhaps he'd expected her to sob, go into hysterics, or perhaps he'd expected her to be so confident of her hold over Noel, she'd dismiss the Spanish girl's problems out of hand. One thing was for sure. He'd felt no pleasure, no sense of vengeance, in telling her.

Gemma sighed. The Scotch must have been a good anaesthetic. Now she felt quite calm.

'I'd better go and speak to both of them,' she said walking to the door aware that Thor had turned and was following her.

'Mr McCabe!' Leo sprang to his feet the moment they entered the sitting-room, his young face contorted with horror and dismay.

'It's OK.' Thor spoke quickly. 'It was a natural misunderstanding. There's no harm done.'

'There's been another misunderstanding too.' Gemma walked towards the chair where the Spanish girl huddled. 'And one for which *I* am entirely to blame.' She took a deep breath, as Josephina raised tear-filled eyes towards her. 'Noel Shelton and I are friends—nothing more. We have never been lovers. We have never planned to be married to each other.'

The pain she was suffering as she tore down her own curtain of lies was worth every pang as she saw hope fill the desolate eyes before her. Bravely she continued. 'A week or so ago—Thor—Mr McCabe—arrived in Menorca. It gave me a shock because I'd known him a long time ago and...' She was conscious of Thor lounging in the doorway, watching her struggles, his face brooding as he drank in every word she uttered. 'I didn't want to establish a close friendship with him again. I—I told him a lie, that I was engaged to be married, without even consulting Noel first. You see, I didn't know he was already committed to you, Josephina. He had been very discreet, obviously because he was deeply in love with you.' Silently, she begged her friend's forgiveness. 'But reluctantly Noel agreed to the deception because he's always been a good friend to me and we didn't think it would be for long...'

'That's what Noel told me!' Excitement replaced despair as Josephina sprang to her feet. 'He said when Mr McCabe had gone back to Australia, he and I would be free to make a formal announcement. If he hadn't...if I hadn't believed him...I would never have...' She broke off, her face flushing with embarrassment as she twisted her fingers together.

There was a poignant silence as Gemma recalled how she herself had trodden the same path, but without the bright future that Josephina's would surely lead to now.

'But you did say you were going to marry him, didn't you?' As if unable to believe the truth, Josephina begged for further reassurance. 'I didn't imagine it, did I? And you did have a ring?'

They were all looking at her, and her ordeal wasn't quite complete.

'Yes,' she said hardly above a whisper. 'Yes, I did say it, but it was never true. The ring was my mother's.' She swallowed, but there was a persisting ache across the bridge of her nose, beneath her eyes. She tried again, knowing it wasn't the admission of her engagement as a pretence that was crucifying her, but the fact of declaring publicly in front of Thor that she was the liar he'd always suspected. 'You see...' she began again.

'What Gemma is trying to tell you is that the final blame is all mine.' Thor walked casually into the centre of the room, hands in trousers pockets, stretching the thin material tightly across his slim hips, striding with the lazy step of a prowling lion, casual, elegant and deadly. 'Because I'm in love with her and I was too arrogant to accept that my feelings weren't returned. I forced my company on her and she accepted it because she believed the future of Noel's plans depended on her co-operation.

'Unfortunately for her, she was in my employ at Tramontana and La Langousta too, and as I'd told her that the continued employment of her friends depended on her goodwill, she felt unable to give in to her natural instincts and smack my face to show how strongly she resented my continued attentions. The story she devised was the only way she saw open to her at the time.' He paused, and for the first time since he'd started speaking he met her troubled regard with a clear, compassionate gaze. 'That's about the long and the short of it, isn't it, Gemma?'

It was too much. The beloved face in front of her swam before her eyes as Gemma made one last determined effort to retain consciousness, then her legs were giving way beneath her as tension and alcohol took their toll. She had one last memory of being lifted before her body reached the floor, of feeling strong arms cradling her body, of savouring the warm, spicy aroma of sweet male flesh before her tired mind found peace in oblivion.

CHAPTER TEN

IN THE golden glow of the Menorcan evening, Gemma watered the last of the several pots of geraniums that made a sweeping band of colour down the steps to the farmhouse door. A background noise of lazy cicadas, mingled with the strains of a Mozart piano concerto from Noel's hi-fi, only added to the melancholy she already felt.

It was hard to realise that only a week had elapsed since Josephina's dramatic performance. A week in which the weather had reverted to its usual mid-season glory, Noel had returned from Barcelona and Thor McCabe and Edmund Curran had put forward fair terms for their investment in the Parangas project, to which Noel had been only too delighted to agree.

Finishing her task, she sank down beside the plants on the steps, offering her golden legs to the last rays of the sun. How she would miss this place when she left. But the time had come for her to find new pastures, and her decision had been only marginally influenced by Noel's impending wedding.

Yes, she thought resignedly, Noel had been right when he'd told her it was time she took another look at her future. Besides, Menorca with all its charm would hold too many memories of Thor now for it to remain the peaceful haven where she'd sought refuge. Having shared so many of her favourite places with him, she knew her future enjoyment of them would always be tempered by the pain of his loss.

170

Reflectively she raised her hand to her cheek. That dreadful night when she'd collapsed and been gathered into his safe embrace, she'd been more exhausted mentally than physically. Unable to fight any more, she'd remained quiescent in his arms as he'd taken her upstairs and laid her down on her virginal single bed with its pristine white bedcover.

Quietly, he'd told her to get some sleep and not to worry. He would stay the night in Noel's room, and if she wanted anything, anything at all, she had only to call his name and he would come to her. Then he had given her a chaste kiss on the cheek and left her. The following morning he'd left at dawn, waiting only long enough to satisfy himself that she was recovered from the trauma of the preceding day. Since then she'd seen or heard nothing from him. The final battle had been hers—and it had brought with it all the lack of joy and satisfaction of a Pyrrhic victory!

'Daydreaming, Gem?'

Noel's light voice disturbed her reflections as he ranged himself alongside her.

'Mmm.' She narrowed her eyes against the copper sky. 'Just sitting here thinking how beautiful it is—how quiet and serene.'

'You don't have to leave it, you know.' He put a friendly hand on her arm. 'Josephina and I are only too happy for you to share the farmhouse with us after we're married.'

'Yes, I know, and I really do appreciate it, but it's time I spread my wings. I'm beginning to stagnate, and the generous gift you've given me has set me free to look for other avenues to explore. I'll stay for your wedding and until the manager Thor's appointed at La Langousta finds a replacement for me, then I'll be packing.'

'I always intended you'd have a share of the capital, Gem.' His fingers squeezed her arm. 'One of the reasons

I didn't tell you about my being in love with Josephina was because I wanted to see you independent first. I guessed how you might feel about sharing, and I didn't want you to think you were being thrown out after all the years of hard work you'd put in.'

'I appreciate your motives, Noel.' She turned her head to smile at him. 'But I wish I *had* known. When I think of the arrogant way I interfered with your life and how Josephina could have died because of it, I feel there's no hole deep enough for me to hide in!'

He shrugged resignedly. 'It's in the past now, and you mustn't blame yourself. I readily agreed to your suggestion for my own selfish reasons, and if Josephina had trusted me a little more she would have waited to face me with her suspicions rather than do what she did. As it is, I owe Leo and you a great debt for being there when I wasn't.'

'And Thor McCabe!' His name rolled off her tongue before she could suppress it. 'He wasn't really involved, but without him...' She shuddered.

'I know.' Noel's heartfelt tone said it all. Into the ensuing silence he added, 'Building starts again at Parangas tomorrow, and I understand the *Brisbane Princess* is pulling up her anchor the day after and heading for North Africa with Thor McCabe aboard.'

'Thor—leaving Menorca already?' The shock made her mouth go dry.

'Why not?' It was a curiously loaded gaze Noel turned on her shocked face. 'What reason does he have to stay here now?'

'None,' Gemma accorded in a small voice. 'And I imagine the charms of the *Brisbane Princess* are a powerful lure.'

'If you mean the yacht, then you may be right. But if you mean what I think you do, I'd say you were wrong. Thor McCabe's had eyes for no other woman than you since he arrived here. Josephina will bear me out on that! She's convinced he's deeply in love with you.'

'And what do *you* think, Noel?' Her voice shook. 'Even supposing that was possible after what I accused him of. You know what happened five years ago, do you think I should take the risk of giving my heart to him a second time?'

'You want the truth?' He watched her nod before continuing, 'I think he's always had it, Gem.'

He was right, of course. That was why she'd never fallen for the charms of other men; why she'd been so disturbed to see him again; why she'd never been able to discourage him as forcefully as she'd wanted to.

She let her dark head drop to her folded arms and stared at the sun-baked ground, only vaguely aware that Noel had risen to his feet.

'I'm on my way to see Josephina down at Tramontana.' The words reached her through a cloud. 'Enjoy your evening off!'

Gemma had been sitting in the darkness of her bedroom for over an hour, the windows wide open, the shutters flung back, watching the stars prick through the dark fabric of the night. The truth of what Noel had said to her was like an indigestible lump sticking in her throat, something she couldn't ignore and hope to go on existing.

Soon, too soon, Thor would have left her life once more, believing she had no feeling left for him, and all because her pride was too brittle to bend a little. He had hurt her once, badly, and she'd tried to hate him, taking a perverse pleasure in pretending to herself that she didn't need him, and all because she'd been too much of a coward to face the truth. She no longer cared that he'd abandoned her five years ago. The past was dead. There might never be a future for them together, but the present was here, now, waiting... What had he said? 'If ever you change your mind, come to me, Gemma, and let me know... I'll be waiting.' As if a dark cloud had lifted from her brain, Gemma knew what she had to do.

Stripping off her casual clothes, she showered before choosing a dress of deep nasturtium orange from her wardrobe; sleeveless and cut high in the bust, it needed no bra. The skirt was full, wrapping round with long ties passing through slits on the waistband. The colour suited her, making her skin gleam golden and her brown eyes soften to a velvet darkness.

Carefully she paid attention to her face, smoothing in a moisturiser on her firm honey skin, thickening the lush sweep of her eyelashes, adding a whisper of sage-green eyeshadow on her pearly lids. The last time Thor had seen her she'd been devoid of make-up, tear-stained, beaten by the elements, her eyes red and swollen. It wasn't how she wanted him to remember her. So she pencilled in the shape of her full, soft mouth with a colour that echoed the shade of her dress, lightly touching the surface in between with a dewy lipstick a shade lighter.

A last look in the mirror persuaded her that she'd never looked better, her soft dark hair forming a glossy frame to her heart-shaped face, her eyes sparkling with the thrill of the challenge she'd set herself. It might not work. Thor could be entertaining or being entertained by the Currans. She might find the Villa Sabina in darkness. But at least she would try.

El Dorado was deserted as she rode down the approach road. For all her purpose, Gemma could feel her courage failing. By the time she'd arrived at the Villa Sabina and seen its empty terrace bathed in a soft light, she was ready to give up her mission. Slowly she walked up the long pathway towards the pool, her heart pounding like a war drum. Suppose he no longer wanted her anyway? Her footsteps slowed down. There was still time to change her mind.

'Gemma?'

Thor came towards her out of the shadows, bathing trunks girding his loins, a towel slung round his neck.

'I heard the scooter; I hoped it might be you.' In the dim light, his eyes were shadowed. 'It was such a hot evening, I was just cooling off in the pool.' He gestured down at himself with a self-deprecating twist of his firm mouth. 'You must think I greet all my guests like this!'

Conscious of his magnetic presence, the lean animal grace of him, Gemma found herself unable to meet his eyes. 'I—I didn't want to intrude.' She swallowed, trying to ease her dry mouth. 'Noel told me you're leaving soon. I wanted to say goodbye.' She stopped, the words sticking in her dry throat.

'I see.' She was conscious of his curiosity. 'Well, we don't want to talk out here, do we? How about coming inside?'

Nodding dumbly, she allowed him to lead the way up the outside stairs on to the flat roof, where he indicated that she sit down on one of the chairs. This was going to be even harder than she'd anticipated! If only she could look at him and tell him what was in her heart, simply open her lips and say, 'I love you.' But the confidence to do so eluded her.

'I'll get some clothes on, Gemma, then I'll rustle us up some coffee. You can amuse yourself by spotting the satellites pass by overhead. I expect you know the heavens in these parts are bursting with them.' He'd gone into the bedroom and his cool voice floated back clearly through the open doors.

'Yes, I know.' She took a deep breath. 'Noel says you're sailing on the *Brisbane Princess* when she leaves.'

'That's right.' Coming to join her, dressed now in white shorts that only covered marginally more of his beauti-

fully balanced frame than the bathing trunks, and
holding a thin cotton shirt in one hand, he subjected her
to a thoughtful stare, as if trying to judge the motive
behind her question.

'The necessary contract for Parangas has been signed
by all concerned parties, except Casados, and we should
receive his signature by tomorrow. After that, there's
nothing here for me to do. Noel's quite capable of or-
ganising the work on the site now he's been relieved of
the money problems.'

'Yes, he is.' She bent her head and gazed down at her
neatly manicured nails. 'He's quite a guy, really. He's
insisted on giving me twenty-five per cent of what you
paid him for the restaurants so I can start up on my own
when he and Josephina get married. I—I thought I'd go
back to England and live with Dad for a while before I
decide what to do next...' She paused, hoping Thor
would speak. When he stayed silent she continued, a
little note of desperation in her voice, 'What about you,
Thor? What plans have you made? Will you go back to
Australia after the cruise?'

'Why did you come here, Gemma? Why did you really
come?' She found her arms seized as he pulled her to
her feet, the shirt he'd been about to put on abandoned
on the hammock. 'It wasn't just to make polite conversation, was it?'

'Thor...' It was a shaky protest at the arbitrary way
he was holding her.

'Was it?' he demanded again hoarsely.

'No.' This was it, the moment of truth, and this time
she wouldn't flinch from it. 'I came because I love you.
Because you asked me to come if I changed my mind.'
She stared into the intense ice-blue of his magnificent
eyes. 'I have changed my mind, Thor. I want you to
make love to me.'

A tremor of fear trembled in her throat as his steady gaze seemed to bore right through her, searching into the secret places of her soul. Suppose he laughed at her, or rejected her—it would be unbearable!

All the old insecurities streamed back into her consciousness as Thor seemed at a loss for words. She'd never understood his violent swing of mood five years ago, had spent hours searching her own behaviour, character, personality, for some flaw that had appeared at the last moment to antagonise him. God knew she wasn't perfect, but she'd failed to identify the fatal blemish in herself that had roused his antipathy. She felt the bitter tears of loss flood her eyes... What if that unknown something had surfaced again to make her undesirable to him? How could she bear this further humiliation?

Wrenching herself away from him, tear-bright eyes fastened to his stunned countenance, she backed towards the open door.

'Gemma, don't! For God's sake, don't cry!' His deep voice was husky, but she was too agitated to recognise the thread of longing in it. She had to escape, to hide her distress in the dark cloak of night. Turning, she ran, but Thor moved so quickly that he'd gained on her as she reached the door from the bedroom into the hallway.

Desperately Gemma seized the handle, feeling the deep sobs hard and repressed inside her chest, only to find that at the moment she opened the door Thor's palm had forced it shut and she was imprisoned between his arms.

'Turn round, Gemma.' It was a command so absolute that she never thought to disobey. Turning in the compass of his arms, she lifted her face towards him, her lips parted and vulnerable. His mouth was incredibly gentle, infinitely desirable, with a promise of hidden passion to come, as it caressed her lips, joined with them and sealed them with a sweetness that calmed her sobs and stilled her tears.

Confined between his body and the door, Gemma lifted her arms, entwining them round his neck. How cool his skin beneath her fevered palms, how erotic its firm smoothness as she moved her hands down his nearly naked body, loving the close texture of the flesh beneath her fingers.

Thor groaned, moving his leg forward, bending the knee so that it parted hers, pinning her to the door by the bright nasturtium cotton of her skirt. Then, and only then, did he take his hands off the door, enfolding her shoulders with his arms, drawing her to him. Their bodies met in intimate delight, her warmth reaching to welcome the cool, commanding power of him, and he swung her round, away from the door, back into the room.

Ardent, searching fingers found the trailing bow that fastened her dress, pulled the ends and caused the glowing cotton to unwind from her shapely hips, to fall open each side of her body, the bodice parting with its weight, revealing her golden, sun-washed breasts unmarked by strap or bikini line.

Thor had stepped back as the material had swirled and divided, and she heard his sharply indrawn breath at the sight of her body naked except for the flowing curtain of cloth still hanging from her shoulders and the flesh-coloured strip of satin that followed the curve of her loins.

Now he closed the slight gap between them again, moulding her towards him, so that the sensitive, expanding tips of her breasts brushed his own, and their fullness flattened against his chest. A shiver of delight ranged through Gemma's throbbing body as the coolness of his skin touched and excited her. As his eager hands stroked the dress from her shoulder, she stepped free of it, entwining her fingers behind Thor's neck, feeling the thick softness of his still-damp hair as she drew his face down to her shoulder.

Warm lips moved against her neck, her throat, nuzzled the firm orbs of her golden breasts, sought pleasure from their tumid peaks, as he swept her up into his arms and carried her the few remaining paces to the bed.

'Oh, my darling girl, I've waited so long to hear you say those words again.' Thor's deep voice trembled with emotion, as he sat down beside her. 'I was suffering the agonies of the damned, believing I'd been given a second chance when it was too late to use it—that you hated me so much I could never overcome your defences.'

'It was never hate, Thor.' Gemma met his gaze without flinching. 'I never stopped loving you, although I nearly managed to persuade myself that I had.' She reached her arms towards him. 'Don't let's talk about the past.'

'We have to, Gemma.' Tenderly he took her out-stretched hands, clasping them between his own two work-roughened palms. 'You have to know why I left you as I did, without a word of kindness or regret. I owe it to you, my darling, and now I know you still love me—I can tell you the truth.'

About to insist that she'd given him her trust with her love, Gemma hesitated. There was such an intense look on Thor's serious face, she knew it would be impossible for them to become lovers again until he'd shriven himself.

Reluctantly she acquiesced. 'Go on.'

For several moments he remained silent, staring down at her hands as they lay in his tender grasp, then he sighed. 'It's difficult to know where to start, but it really goes back sixteen years to when we moved to Melbourne, and I got interested in power-boat racing.'

'I remember you telling me...' Gemma nodded encouragingly. 'That was when you were in that terrible accident where you got the cut over your eye...'

'And was badly concussed for nearly a week. Yes.' He raised his eyes to meet her enquiring gaze. 'The doctors said at the time I was lucky to be alive. One of the crew died when the boat exploded and the other lost a leg, but apart from a relatively minor cut it seemed I'd escaped scot-free.'

'Thor?' A dreadful premonition made icy fingers clench round her heart, squeezing the warmth from her body. 'What are you telling me? That they were mistaken...that there *is* something wrong with you? Oh, my darling love...' She read something of the truth on his face and, releasing her hands flung them round his shoulders, hugging him to her. 'You should have told me! Whatever it is, we can face it together, Thor. Did you really think it would make any difference to the way I felt about you?'

'No, I didn't, Gemma.' He spoke softly, caressing the satin skin of her back, as his cheek brushed her own. 'And that was the real problem. You see, shortly after coming to England I began to get pains in the head, localised and very intense. I guess I must have had some premonition because I went directly to a London specialist, and after X-rays and a brain scan he gave me the unvarnished truth—I'd better not make any long-term plans.'

'What are you saying?' Ashen-faced, she wrenched herself away, perspiration forming a cold mist on her forehead as the import of his words sank into her numbed brain.

'Gemma, Gemma, my love. It's all right.' He drew her trembling body back into his embrace. 'I'm saying that I'm one hundred per cent fit, that I'll probably live to a hundred...now.'

'It was a mistake, then?' she asked shakily.

'No. It seems that, although it was undetected in the X-rays after the accident, there was a bone splinter that had penetrated into my brain. For years it lay dormant, causing no trouble, then apparently it began to move.' He shrugged. 'No one knows exactly why, but I took a few tumbles playing football over the years and that might have been enough. By the time I got the headaches it had become inoperable. The prognosis, as they say, was negative.'

'And you never told me!' She shivered, her fertile imagination guessing at his shock and fear and anger.

'How could I, Gemma? I loved you too much to allow you to waste all your love and compassion on a dying man. I didn't want your pity. I didn't want to become like the poor little finch you cradled in your hand and willed back to life, because there was no chance you could will me back to life and I didn't want you to remember me as weak and in pain!' His voice broke agonisingly, and Gemma could only cling to his broad shoulders, waiting for him to regain self-control. A few seconds passed, with only his harsh breathing breaking the stillness of the room, then he continued quietly, 'Neither did I want you to mourn me. You were so young, so full of life and love, so tender-hearted. I was afraid you might devote yourself to my memory instead of finding another lover who could bring you joy and the fulfilment you deserved. Don't you see—because I loved you I wanted to set you free, and the only way I could think of doing it was to kill every vestige of love you had for me?

'Yes, I knew I was hurting you, but in the circumstances it seemed the kindest thing to do. I prayed your love would turn to hate and that hate would cauterise the pain I'd caused you, so you would begin to live your life again, free of my memory.'

'So you told me you no longer loved me, that it had only been a physical attraction . . .' She gulped down her rising tears. 'And you went back to Australia to die at home with your family...'

'To die alone, Gemma,' he corrected harshly. 'No one could say exactly how much time I had, but it was weeks or months, not years. I'd always been so active that I was determined not to just lie down in a bed and wait for the end, so that's when I joined a gang of cattle musterers. It was tough and hard and it suited me just fine.' He gave a short laugh. 'At least if I had to die, I'd go like a man, in the saddle!' He paused while Gemma waited, holding her breath. 'It turned out to be the best possible thing I could have done, because a few weeks after starting I suffered a particularly bad attack and parted company with my horse, breaking my neck in the process.'

'Dear God!' It was a prayer breathed from her barely parted lips. 'I can't believe this!'

'Oh, believe it, my love, because this is where the miracle happened. I was taken to the hospital unconscious and partly paralysed. Of course, routine X-rays were taken and the splinter's existence identified, but this time the trauma of the accident had caused it to shift once again. I was told that there was a very good chance now of an operation to remove it being totally successful.'

'And it was—totally?' Eagerly, Gemma begged him to confirm it.

'Absolutely.' He smiled at her. 'It was a long haul to complete recovery, though. For six months I was so down I almost wished I had died!'

'You should have sent for me, Thor!' Gemma protested angrily. 'I would have come to you. Surely you knew that!'

'Yes, I knew it. And what would you have found? An invalid with wasted muscles and a shaven head! Do you think I would have wanted you to see me like that? No,

Gemma. I'd deliberately set you free, and the last thing I wanted was to use your capacity for compassion to bring you back to me.'

'You were so wrong...' Gemma swallowed back her tears, appalled at the suffering he'd undergone, but unwilling to chide him too severely. 'So dreadfully, dreadfully wrong...'

'Not by my standards, sweetheart.' He bent his head to place a gentle kiss on her shoulder. 'But when I got on the mend, when I could start to repair the ravages of idleness on my body, when I could look in a mirror and see once more the Thor McCabe who once seriously considered playing professional football...then I knew I was going after the only thing in the world I really wanted—you.'

'You—you mean, it's taken you five years to get fit again?'

'Just over one,' he returned sombrely, meeting her puzzled gaze with his clear blue regard.

'But...' Gemma paused. 'I don't understand...'

'As soon as I'd made my mind up to try and win you back again, I phoned your home in England and spoke to your father. He told me you were abroad. Naturally, I asked for your address, but he said you were touring, so I told him I would write to you in England if he would pass the letter to you as soon as you were settled.' His firm lips moved in a rueful smile. 'He promised he would.'

'A letter? But I never received a letter from you!' Gemma's brow wrinkled in puzzlement. 'And I never toured. I went straight to Mahón...'

'Yes, I know that now, because when I went back to England for my grandmother's funeral your father and I got talking. When I told him the whole story he was anguished with guilt. You see, when I'd phoned him from Oz he'd no idea of what had happened, and his one thought was to protect you from me. He told me he'd seen how much you'd grieved for me, and no way was he going to allow me back into your life again at a point where you were just beginning to get over my betrayal. So he took it on himself to destroy my letter.'

'Oh, Thor, how could he?' she moaned, yet she knew the answer.

'It was because he loved you so dearly.' Thor confirmed her own opinion. 'When he heard all the facts he was distraught. That was when he told me how at the beginning of your life your natural mother put you up for adoption so she could marry her current lover, and how cruelly that rejection had affected you. He swore that he and his wife had always done everything in their power to make you feel needed and loved—which indeed you were—and how bitterly angry they'd been when I walked out on you, although for your sake they'd tried to minimise the outward expression of their outrage.' He touched her cheek gently with his forefinger. 'He was full of remorse, Gemma. Furious as I was, I couldn't condemn him, and it will break his heart if you can't find it within yourself to forgive him...'

'Of course I forgive him!' Her dark eyes glowed. 'He acted for what he thought was the best—and he did admit his involvement when he realised he'd been wrong in his judgement of you.'

Thor nodded. 'That wasn't an easy thing to do. At the time I felt like punching him on the jaw; it was only the thought that one day he might be my father-in-law that stopped me!'

Gemma smiled at his wry humour, her thoughts in turmoil as she tried to assimilate everything she'd been told. 'What did you write to me in your letter, Thor?' she asked wistfully, remembering how unhappy she had been four years ago.

'Just the truth. Everything that had happened. My reasons for leaving you and my reasons for wanting to see you.' His voice softened. 'Of course, I couldn't be sure that you'd ever want to set eyes on me again. A year had passed and there could easily have been someone else. So I said that if you still loved me just let me know, and I would come anywhere in the world to meet you and marry you! But that if I didn't hear from you I'd know I'd lost you.'

'If I'd only known...' Gemma dropped her head forwards so it lay on Thor's golden shoulder, shuddering as she envisaged the mental and physical torture he'd survived. 'But, if you still felt the same way when you came to Menorca, why didn't you tell me straight away?'

His sigh was a sweet breath against her skin. 'Five years, Gemma... It was a long time. There was always the possibility that we'd grown too far apart, as you yourself insisted, and the last thing I wanted was to tell you the truth and have you mistake surprise and pity for a defunct love! I had to get to know you again, to find out for myself whether any embers still burnt in your heart for me... Besides,' he exhaled a deep breath, 'I'd promised your father that I wouldn't reveal his part in all this unless it was absolutely necessary. And then, of course, you sprang Noel on me.'

'Poor Noel,' Gemma smiled. 'I treated him appallingly, abusing his friendship and nearly ruining his business prospects under the guise of helping him!'

'Dear God, yes, Gemma!' he admitted heartfeltedly. 'I was bitterly jealous of Noel. I'd known from the moment you walked out of Tramontana that night that I still loved you, and my instinct was to try and rout him out of your life, but I'd no wish to hurt you again, and perhaps you did care for him. Although I never could quite believe, despite the act you put on, that you'd

changed so much you'd let one man make love to you
while you wore another man's ring.'

'I was afraid to let you see how much I did love you,'
she confessed quietly. 'It was such a shock, seeing you
again and realising how desperately I still wanted you.
But I'd convinced myself anything between us would only
be temporary...' She gave a little sob. 'I've been so
stupid, Thor, so blindly stubborn, only concerned with
my own pride; and then tonight I knew you'd been right.
It's not often in life that fate gives you a second bite at
the cherry, and I knew if I let you leave Menorca without
telling you how much I love you and asking you to love
me again, I'd regret it all my life.'

Thor's amused chuckle relieved some of her tension.
'You put up a marvellous, spirited fight, my darling.
That last night at the farmhouse, I truly believed every
word I said to Josephina. I thought I'd lost you for ever.
If you hadn't come to me tonight, I would have gone
back to Australia and never bothered you again.'

'My sweet, sweet love...' As Thor lowered his head
to find the thrusting beauty of her naked breasts with
his questing lips, Gemma sighed in deepest pleasure, her
hand rising to touch his chest, the thumb moving hard
against his flesh, feeling the resistance of the strong, firm
wedge of abdominal muscle until it rested on the clasp
of his shorts.

She felt the shiver of anticipation that trembled
through his strong frame as he lifted her in his arms,
cradling her against him and looking down into her upturned face. The moonlight flirted with his image,
darkened the hollows in his cheeks and temples, highlighted the broad sweep of his forehead, the tender curl
of his sensuous mouth and the liquid softness of his de-
siring eyes.

His mouth caressed her, seeking her lips as if it had
no purpose save to touch, to taste her, to become a part

of her, and Gemma understood implicitly everything he wanted to tell her and could find no words for.

Reaching for him, she felt his body as if she were blind and would imprint its image on her mind never to be forgotten. Moving erotically against him while her body sang and vibrated beneath his tender hands and persuasive mouth, she re-enacted the scenes of her youth, slowly and unerringly bringing Thor to a pitch of physical response that had him groaning her name.

But there was one last thing. One last confession she must make to put the record straight while he was still able to comprehend it.

'My darling Thor,' her voice was languid with passion, 'I lied to you when I said there had been other men. You were my only love...my only lover.'

'You told so many lies, sweetheart.' His smile robbed the words of reproach. 'But there was one outstanding truth, although you didn't dream it at the time!'

'Mmm?' She was in no mood for guessing games.

'You told me you were getting married this coming October in the parish church at Leychurch.'

'And I am?' For a moment she was roused from her lethargy by the promise of such an ecstatic future.

'Oh, yes, sweet Gemma...I guarantee it!'

Suddenly her body was a core of white-hot energy crying out for Thor to claim and contain it, and she was whimpering, small, inarticulate sounds of pleasure and pleading as he rolled away for a breathless second. When he rejoined her there was nothing between them except the mingled dew of their skins, and as Gemma welcomed Thor back to herself with great pleasure, taking him and enjoying him as she had never dared hope to again, she lifted him with her, taking them both to the threshold of fulfilment—and beyond.

In that room of moonlight and shadow, she lay curled up against him, her head against his shoulder. There had been a long, unbroken silence following the glorious climax of their union. At last Thor propped himself up on one elbow, his gaze tender and admiring, sweeping up the long length of Gemma's body before coming to rest on her face.

'If it takes me the rest of my life, I mean to make it up to you for all the heartache I've caused you,' he vowed determinedly.

She smiled at his anxious expression. 'Dear Thor, you already have. And just think what a story we'll have to tell our children!'

She heard his soft, appreciative laugh, felt his arms close in tender affection around her exhausted body and sighed with deep contentment. It had taken five years, but love's wrongs had finally been righted and all was well with her world at last.

You'll flip . . . your pages won't!
Read paperbacks *hands-free* with

Book Mate • I

The perfect "mate" for all your romance paperbacks

Traveling • Vacationing • At Work • In Bed • Studying • Cooking • Eating

Perfect size for all standard paperbacks, this wonderful invention makes reading a pure pleasure! Ingenious design holds paperback books OPEN and FLAT so even wind can't ruffle pages — leaves your hands free to do other things. Reinforced, wipe-clean vinyl-covered holder flexes to let you turn pages without undoing the strap . . . supports paperbacks so well, they have the strength of hardcovers!

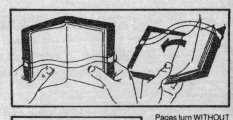

Pages turn WITHOUT opening the strap.

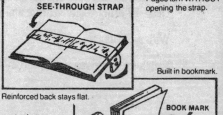

SEE-THROUGH STRAP

Reinforced back stays flat.

Built in bookmark.

BOOK MARK

BACK COVER HOLDING STRIP

10" x 7¼", opened.
Snaps closed for easy carrying, too.

BARBARA DELINSKY

THROUGH MY EYES

Smuggled diamonds . . . a desperate search for answers . . . a consuming passion that wouldn't be denied . . .

This May, Harlequin Temptation and Barbara Delinsky bring you adventure and romance . . .

With a difference . . .

Watch for this riveting book from Temptation.

HARLEQUIN *Temptation*

Harlequin American Romance

Romances that go one step farther...
American Romance

Realistic stories involving people you can relate to and care about.

Compelling relationships between the mature men and women of today's world.

Romances that capture the core of genuine emotions between a man and a woman.

Join us each month for four new titles wherever paperback books are sold.
Enter the world of American Romance.

Harlequin Superromance

Here are the longer, more involving stories you have been waiting for . . . Superromance.

Modern, believable novels of love, full of the complex joys and heartaches of real people.

Intriguing conflicts based on today's constantly changing life-styles.

Four new titles every month.
Available wherever paperbacks are sold.

Keepsake

 Harlequin Books

You're never too young to enjoy romance. Harlequin for you . . . and Keepsake, young-adult romances destined to win hearts, for your daughter.

Pick one up today and start your daughter on her journey into the wonderful world of romance.

Two new titles to choose from each month.